Dances with the Dirt

By

Harry Albino

Dedication

I want to dedicate this book to my mother Genevieve. The children Vincent, Jeremy, Damian and Bobby. A Special dedication to Lena Rumfelt and Erik Hernandez for their inspiration. And to those others who believed in me. And a Spcial dedication to Rachel, the woman who raised the four children. Thank you.

Harry Albino

Acknowledgment

Special acknowledgement to Rafael Santana, the actual shortstop of the 1986 Mets. Although the story is fictional, some of the baseball facts are real. Here's to hoping that time hasn't forgotten these great players.

About the Author

Harry Albino was born in 1962 on Manhattan's Lower East Side. He was raised in the housing projects. In 1981, he was arrested as a suspect in a murder and assault. In March of 1982, Albino was acquitted of murder, but convicted of manslaughter in the second and third degrees, assault in the second and third degree. However, in 1984, his manslaughter in the third degree and assault in the third degree were overturned. While incarcerated, Mr. Albino earned his GED, an Associates Degree and a Bachelors Degree. He was paroled in 1987. He worked in Graphic Arts for five years and in healthcare for twenty-five years. Mr. Albino retired in 2018. This is his first novel.

Prologue: The Interview

November 1st, 2027 — Miami, Florida

The sun was dripping low over Biscayne Bay, casting long shadows across the studio windows of a modest recording space tucked behind a Cuban café.

Sonny "Mercury" Mercado adjusted his mic, checked his notes, and glanced at the clock. He had been a fighter once, lightweight division. Quick hands, quicker wit. But after the gloves came off, baseball became his new ring. His podcast, *The Mercury Temperature*, began as a niche passion project. Over time, it evolved into a widely respected platform, beloved by listeners who craved stories as much as stats, narratives that dug deeper than box scores and batting averages.

Today's guest was different.

Today, he wasn't just interviewing a player. He was welcoming a myth.

Jervin Class.

A potential Hall of Famer. Known as the Architect of the infield, a master of defensive fielding prowess. Sonny had waited years for this sit-down. Jervin rarely did interviews. He preferred silence to spectacle. But something about Sonny's style, his grit, his reverence, had opened the door.

Sonny stood.

"Jervin Class. Welcome to *The Mercury Temperature*."

Jervin nodded. "Good to be here, Sonny."

They shook hands. It was firm, respectful. The kind of handshake that said, *I know where you've been.*

"So, Jervin," Sonny began, settling into his chair. "Tell us how your road began."

Jervin paused. The mic picked up the soft creak of his chair as he leaned back, eyes narrowing not in discomfort, but in memory.

"You ever hear a ball hitting a back alley?" he said. "Not a bat. Just a broomstick. That's how it started. The Lower East Side. 1968. My brother Manny and I used to play stickball between tenement buildings. We didn't have gloves, just calloused hands and dreams that felt too big for the block we lived on."

Sonny didn't speak. He let the silence stretch, knowing it was sacred. The kind of silence that held more truth than any stat line.

"We used chalk for bases. Sewer caps for home plate," Jervin continued. "Manny was faster than me, but I had the hands. I could scoop a ball off cracked concrete like it was velvet. That's where I learned angles and anticipation. You don't wait for the ball in the street. You meet it."

He smiled, just barely.

"We used to pretend we were the Mets. Cleon Jones, Bud Harrelson, Ed Charles. Manny always wanted to be Tommie Agee. Said he liked the way he flew."

Sonny leaned forward, eyes gleaming. "You ever think you'd make it out?"

"Not at first. But then I saw how the game could bend time. How it could make a kid from the projects feel like he belonged in the big leagues. That feeling? That's what I chased."

Jervin's voice softened.

"My father worked weekend nights at the Brooklyn Navy Yard. He came home smelling like steel and sweat. He didn't say much, but on Sundays, for a while, he'd take us to Shea Stadium. We had upper-deck seats, the nosebleeds. It didn't matter. That was our religion. Baseball."

He paused, eyes distant.

"I remember watching Cleon Jones track a fly ball like it was destiny. That's when I knew I didn't want to be famous. I wanted to be essential. The kind of player who made the play that kept the inning alive. The guy who turned two when no one thought it was possible."

Sonny nodded. "You weren't chasing the spotlight. You were chasing rhythm."

"Exactly," Jervin said. "Baseball's a symphony, Sonny. And I wanted to be second violin, the one that held the harmony together."

Sonny leaned back, letting the words settle like dust after a double play.

"That's the kind of thinking that doesn't show up in the highlight reels," he said. "But it's what makes legends."

Jervin chuckled, low and dry. "Legends are for people who need stories. I just needed the game."

He glanced at the studio window, where the last light over Biscayne Bay flickered like stadium lights in the distance.

"You know what I miss the most?" he said. "Not the roar. Not the stats. It's the quiet between pitches. That breath before the ball leaves the pitcher's hand. That's where the truth lives."

Sonny scribbled again, but slower now. He wasn't just recording a podcast. He was witnessing a confession.

"You ever think about going back?" Sonny asked. "Coaching, maybe?"

Jervin's eyes darkened, not with anger, but with something older. Regret. Or reverence.

"I think about Manny," he said. "About the plays we never got to finish. That's what I'd go back for."

Sonny paused, his pen hovering above the page.

"So, what happened to Manny?"

Jervin's eyes dropped for the first time. His voice, when it came, was steady but hollowed out.

"Manny joined the Marines when he was eighteen. Tough kid. That was '79. After basic training, he was deployed to Germany. One day, he was driving on the Autobahn. Car accident. He was killed instantly."

"I never knew that," Sonny said quietly.

"I stopped thinking about it so I wouldn't go crazy," Jervin replied. "But if I've got one regret in this life…" He looked up, his voice catching. "It's that he never saw me play."

Act 1: The Right Field Revelation

Sonny leaned in, mic steady.

"So, Jervin, when did you first play baseball, besides stickball, with other kids?"

Jervin smiled, eyes drifting back.

"It was around '72 or '73. I was ten or eleven. We had this teacher, George. I never knew his last name. Just George. Young guy, mid-twenties or so. Tall, slim, muscular. Full of energy. He wasn't like the other teachers. He talked to us like we mattered."

He paused, letting the memory settle.

"One day, we had this outdoor sporting event in the schoolyard. The gym teacher picked teams, and they stuck me in right field. I didn't think much of it. I wasn't a natural athlete. I was quiet, kept to myself. Good grades. Most kids called me a nerd."

Sonny chuckled softly.

"For some reason," Jervin continued, "the other kids thought I could play that day. They saw something I didn't. To me, it was just luck. A matter of chance."

Sonny leaned in closer.

"So, what happened next?"

Jervin's voice softened.

"A ball was hit high, slicing toward the fence. I tracked it, gloved it, and snagged it clean. No bobble. No stumble. Just instinct."

He smiled, the kind that comes from remembering something sacred.

The yard went quiet for a second. Then it erupted. One kid yelled, "Yo, Class can play!" I didn't know what to do. I just smiled, for the first time that week.

George came over after the game, clipboard tucked under his arm, eyes sharp.

He asked me, "You ever think about joining the Boys Club on 10th Street?"

"I didn't," Jervin said. "It was the furthest thing from my mind. Organized baseball. That was for kids with cleats and parents who clapped from the bleachers. Not for me. Not for Manny and me."

He paused again, voice steady.

"But that day, right field, chalk lines, the echo of a clean catch, that was the first time I played any sort of organized ball. And for the first time, I belonged."

Sonny leaned in.

"That was the moment, huh? When the game found you?"

Jervin nodded.

"Yeah. I didn't chase baseball. It found me in right field."

Act 2: The Cage and the Contact

The Boys Club on 10th Street smelled like linoleum, old sweat, and ambition.

The batting cage was tucked in the back, behind the ping-pong tables and the trophy case filled with dust and forgotten names. Jervin stood there, eleven years old, holding a bat that felt too big for his hands.

George was there, clipboard again, watching without pressure.

"Just swing. Don't think. Feel," George said.

The first few pitches were wild. Jervin missed. Swung late. Swung early. But then he made contact. A clean crack. The ball ricocheted off the netting like a promise.

George smiled. "That's it. That's the sound."

Jervin didn't say anything. But inside, something shifted. The cage wasn't a trap. It was a temple. And the contact? That was communion.

Before George refilled the machine, he stepped into the cage with Jervin. No clipboard. No ego. Just a guy who cared.

"Put your feet even with the plate," George said. "Keep the bat over the zone, arms back. Don't lunge. You're not trying to crush it. You're trying to make contact. Put the ball in play. And the most important thing, keep your eyes on the ball."

Jervin adjusted. Took a breath.

The next pitch came in clean, fast, humming with possibility.

Jervin connected. Not a bomb, but a crisp line drive into right-center. Then another. And another. Jervin rarely missed. His hits weren't loud. They were smooth. Steady. Like he'd found a rhythm that had been waiting for him.

George didn't say anything after that. He just nodded, refilled the machine, and let him keep swinging.

Jervin finished multiple rounds in the cage. He remembered the sting in his hands, the taste of dust in the air. But with every swing of the bat, doubt faded. In its place came rhythm. Confidence. Not loud or boastful, but steady. Earned.

George watched quietly, letting the silence hold Jervin's own discovery. He didn't need to say a word. The echo of each hit lingered, not just in the cage, but somewhere deeper. A place only courage reaches when it's given permission.

That day, Jervin started to understand baseball wasn't just a game. It was a language. And for the first time, he was fluent.

His hands stopped trembling. His stance felt natural. He wasn't swinging. He was hitting.

George stood behind the cage, arms crossed, nodding. No clipboard. No corrections.

Just presence.

"You're ready, kid," George said.

That moment changed everything.

Jervin wasn't just a kid with a glove anymore. He was a ballplayer. And George? He was the first person who saw that in Jervin.

Sonny leaned forward, voice low. "George is the kind of coach who changes lives. Not just swings."

Jervin nodded. "Exactly. He didn't just teach me how to hit. He taught me how to believe."

Act 3: The Ride Home

The batting cages were silent now. The machines had stopped, their metallic rhythm replaced by the low hum of George's Buick as we rolled toward Delancey Street. Twilight was setting in, the sky bruised with fading light, and I knew I needed to get home before my parents started to worry.

George kept both hands steady on the wheel, his eyes fixed on the road ahead. I turned to him.

"George… what's your last name?"

Without missing a beat, he said, "Weinstein."

I blinked. "Weinstein? I didn't know you were Jewish."

George chuckled, still watching the traffic. "Well, I'm not a practicing Jew. I just happen to have the last name Weinstein."

I leaned back, chewing on it. "I always thought you were Italian."

George glanced at me, amused. "Why is that?"

"I don't know," I said. "The other day I heard you say, 'We have tree kids that need tutoring in math.' The only people I know who say *tree* instead of *three* are the guys on the corner in my neighborhood who take numbers. You know, guys named Vinny."

George grinned.

"Not a bookie. Just a guy who knows a guy," I said.

George shook his head, still smiling.

"Kid, accents don't come with birth certificates. They come with sidewalks."

As the car slowed near my building, something caught my eye, a stack of books in the back seat, their spines thick and worn. I turned my head quickly.

"George, what are those books?"

He glanced in the rearview mirror. "Law books."

I blinked. "You studying to be a lawyer?"

George shrugged. "Something like that."

I grinned. "You planning on representing half my neighborhood?"

George laughed, that dry chuckle of his. "No. I don't want to be a criminal lawyer. I want to help people when they sign contracts, so they don't get fleeced."

I nodded, not fully understanding, but liking the sound of it. Just as he said that, the car slowed to a stop.

"Okay, you're home," George said.

I grabbed my glove and opened the door. "Thank you, George. Or should I say, Mr. Weinstein."

George laughed.

He watched me walk toward my building, backpack slung over one shoulder, glove dangling from the other. And he wondered how a kid living in the projects could still smile like that. Still say thank you as if it were second nature.

George had been raised middle class. He grew up with resources. He chose teaching. Chose mentoring. Chose to be present for kids who did not always have that kind of support. He did not need to say it out loud, but he felt it deep in his chest.

This is why I do it, he concluded.

Act 4: Right Field and Clemente

Sonny smiled and leaned forward.

"So, tell us what happened next?"

Jervin's eyes softened with fondness.

"I started Little League that summer. Met a bunch of kids my age, but one stood out. Junior. Junior was bigger than me, a year older, and carried an aura like he could kick serious ass."

He smiled.

"We hit it off right away. I was a shy kid. He was a mouthy kid. I guess opposites really do attract."

He paused, remembering.

"Later on, we found out both our mothers attended Seward Park High School. They both graduated in 1959. That felt like fate nudging us together."

I wanted to be near him. Maybe so he could ward off the bullies. More than that, I appreciated having someone who understood me.

My first game, the coach put me in right field. I didn't care. I was just happy to be on the field.

First at bat, I made contact. The ball took off like it had somewhere to be.

"Holy shit," I muttered under my breath.

"Run! What are you doing?" the coach screamed in his thick New York accent.

I was admiring the shot so much that I forgot to run. But I was fast, and I ended up with a triple.

Suddenly, I could smell the grass, the dirt, the sweat on my brow. It was alive. I was having a blast.

A couple of my uncles showed up to watch me play. They were alcoholics. One of them carried a transistor radio, the kind that buzzed with static and Mets scores.

Later in the game, a ball was hit to right field. I scooped it up, emulating Roberto Clemente, my hero. Planting my feet, I fired a strike to third. Nailed the runner trying to advance from first to third.

My uncles went nuts.

"That's my nephew! That's the next Roberto Clemente!" they shouted.

I felt embarrassed. But also proud.

Still, something gnawed at me. The other kids had their mothers, fathers, or siblings in the stands. I never did. My parents were around. Sort of. But not in the bleachers. Not cheering. Not seeing.

Manny had moved to Pennsylvania with my grandparents. I was a lonely child, with few friends. For my parents, Little League was just a summer pastime.

But for me, it was a shot at something. A long shot, sure, but still hope.

It was something to hold on to when everything else felt slippery.

Act 5: The Hallways of Another World

Sonny was silent. His voice, almost cracking, finally broke through.

"So... you went to middle school, through high school, at an Ivy League–level private school on a scholarship. Tell us about that."

Jervin paused. His voice was steady, but there was weight behind it.

"Yeah. It sounds crazy, right? A kid from the housing projects suddenly walking through marble hallways and mahogany doors.

It wasn't Ivy League in the college sense, but it was one of those elite prep schools. The kind where the kids wore blazers, and their parents wore power."

It happened because of a scholarship. One of my teachers, Ms. Alvarez, saw something in me and recommended me after I scored in the 90th percentile and carried a high average in math. She said I had potential beyond baseball. I didn't really understand what she was implying. Baseball was my dream. But I did like to read.

The next thing I knew, I was sitting in classrooms where kids talked about summer homes and ski trips. Meanwhile, I felt lucky just to have gone to Great Adventure.

I wore sneakers that were wearing out and carried a Mets folder held together with duct tape along the spine.

Jervin paused, then continued.

"It was tough. I didn't fit in. I didn't talk much. I ate lunch alone for the first few weeks. But I listened. I watched. I learned how to adapt to an environment that wasn't built for me."

The teachers were mostly kind. Others weren't. They found subtle ways to remind me who I was and where I came from.

"One day, a classmate asked me if I lived in a regular building or government housing."

I just said, "I live where people work hard and stay genuine."

"I didn't fight. I didn't yell. I just kept showing up. Kept getting A's. Kept playing ball after school with Junior and the guys back home.

I gained ground at that school. Not just in literature and math. I learned about code-switching. About survival. About how to carry your roots into places that don't understand your soil."

I didn't belong there. But I didn't let that stop me from learning everything I could.

Sonny said softly, his voice almost reverent, "That's not just education. That's armor."

Jervin nodded.

"Exactly. I didn't go there to become someone else. I went there to sharpen who I already was."

Act 6: The Dream Behind the Counter

Dances with the Dirt

Sonny leaned forward, curious.

"Okay, so how did you handle finances?"

Jervin smiled, his voice steady.

"I worked after school that first year. I needed money for books, bus fare, and a little something to help at home. So I got a job at a sporting goods store. Junior worked there too and recommended me."

It wasn't glamorous. We stacked shelves, rang up customers, swept floors. But we liked it. We were around gear, around the game. Gloves, bats, cleats. It felt like we were touching pieces of the dream.

One slow Tuesday, Junior and I were behind the counter doing inventory. He looked up and said,

"Yo, Jervin… how much you think it costs to start one of these?"

I laughed. "What, a store?"

"Yeah," he said. "Like, if we saved up. Got a loan. You think it's profitable?"

I shrugged. "I don't know. But we could dream, right?"

It was silly. But it was ours.

The store became more than a job. It became a workshop for hope. A place where we talked about life, about baseball, about getting out, without forgetting where we came from.

Sonny smiled.

"That's the kind of dream that sticks. Not just for profit, but for purpose."

Jervin nodded.

"Exactly. We didn't want to just sell gear. We wanted to build something that felt like a home. A brand."

Act 7: Dancing with the Dirt

Sonny leaned in, eyes wide.

"So what happened the next year?"

Jervin grinned, his voice tinged with wonder.

"That summer, everything started to move. I was still working at the sporting goods store, but on weekends, I played hardball. For the first time, I started playing shortstop. I was raw, but hungry."

One Saturday, after a tight game, this Dominican guy walks up to me. Built like a tank. Eyes sharp. He says, "You know, you're throwing the ball wrong."

I was shocked. I mean, who says that to a stranger?

He noticed my discomfort and invited me to his game on Sunday. "Game starts at three. I'll show you how."

I thought to myself, this guy is arrogant, but sure of himself. You never know.

"So I went to his game on Sunday, like he said. And holy shit, this guy was a monster. He played third base like it was sacred ground. He could hit, field, and his arm was a cannon.

But it wasn't brute force. It was technique. Footwork. Timing. Balance. He didn't just throw. He delivered. Like every toss had a purpose. A story.

I watched him for four innings before he approached me. He walked over, glove in hand, and handed me a ball.

'Now you try.'

Before I threw, he asked, 'What did you notice about my throws?'

I said, 'You used your wrist. Generated more power.'

He nodded. 'Correct. But it's not just that. It's footwork. It's rhythm. Like dancing with the dirt.'

That line stuck with me. Dancing with the dirt."

He showed me how each step set up the throw. How balance created velocity. It wasn't just mechanics. It was music.

I started practicing in front of a mirror every night. Footwork. Wrist snap. Posture. I wasn't just throwing. I was releasing. Because my goal was to try out for my school's team the following year.

That summer, everything changed. I wasn't just playing ball anymore. I was learning the language of the game.

Sonny said softly, "That's when it became real, huh?"

Jervin laughed.

"Yeah. That's when I stopped playing and started becoming."

Sonny leaned in, curious.

"So did you ever find out the Dominican guy's name? And what was his interest?"

Jervin smiled, his voice tinged with memory.

"Yeah, Sonny, I did. His name was Rafael. Rafael Blanco. He told me later he used to play semi-pro ball back in the Dominican Republic, though his English suggested he was raised in New York. He worked construction during the week and played on Sundays like it was sacred."

His interest? It wasn't about scouting or anything like that. He just loved the game. Said it kept him sane. Said it reminded him of home. And he said I reminded him of a younger version of himself. He was ten years older than me.

Sonny said quietly, "That's the kind of man who leaves fingerprints on your soul."

Jervin nodded.

"Exactly. He taught me how to throw. But more than that, he taught me how to carry myself. And most of all, how to dance with the dirt."

Act 8: The Tryout

Dances with the Dirt

Sonny leaned in, voice steady.

"Let's talk about your tryout."

Jervin smiled, eyes narrowing with memory.

"It was the spring of 1978. I was a couple of weeks shy of my sixteenth birthday. When I first started at that school, I had nothing. No gear. No name. Just a dream and a quiet fire.

But I was working at the sporting goods store, and Jerry, the owner, he saw the desire in me. One day I told him I had a tryout coming up. He didn't blink. Just said, 'Pick what you need. We'll deduct it from your paycheck. I want you to kick ass.'"

Tryout day came. I showed up with a new glove, cleats that fit, and a bat that didn't feel like a broomstick. I still felt like an outsider, but I looked like I belonged.

The field was pristine. Chalk lines sharp, the diamond gleaming under the spring sun. A far cry from the pebble-ridden infields of the Lower East Side.

The bleachers were filled with parents, siblings, and students in varsity jackets.

I stretched alone. No one knew my name. But there wasn't a name on the clipboard for me yet. I was there to be undeniable.

The coach ran us through drills. Grounders. Double plays. Pop flies. Every simulation meant to mirror real action. I played shortstop the way Rafael taught me. Footwork tight. Throws crisp.

I didn't try to show off. I just made the routine look beautiful.

Then came batting practice. I stepped to the plate, heart pounding. The first pitch came fast. I fouled it off.

On the second pitch, I connected. Line drive to right-center. Third pitch, same thing. The ball looked different to me now, like it carried its own light.

The coach nodded. "Okay. Go to short. Let's see what you have in live batting practice."

That's when I knew it wasn't just a tryout anymore. It was an audition for belief. And every swing, every step, every throw was another line in my story.

Jerry's words echoed in my head. *Kick ass.*

Sonny was grinning.

"That's the kind of moment that separates the dreamers from the doers."

Jervin nodded.

"Yeah. That day, I stopped dreaming and started proving."

He paused, leaned back, his voice shifting.

"Of course, Sonny… that tryout didn't come without a caveat."

Sonny leaned in.

"Like?"

Jervin laughed, recalling the incident.

"There was this one kid, Brandon. Legacy player. His dad was on the board. His uncle coached at Columbia. He'd played shortstop the year before. Smooth hands. Good instincts. But he saw me as a threat."

Jervin smiled.

"You ever see *Back to School* with Rodney Dangerfield?"

Sonny grinned. "Yeah. Funny movie."

Jervin nodded. "Remember the bully on the swim team?"

Sonny laughed. "Yeah. He was kind of a douche."

Jervin smirked. "Brandon was a carbon copy. Same smug face. Same cheap shots. It's like they based that character on him."

He kept tossing little remarks my way. Called me a "Punch and Judy hitter." Said I couldn't drive the ball if my life depended on it.

Two swings later, I hit three consecutive home runs.

The first sailed over the left-field fence.

The second cleared center field, straight away.

The third was a bomb, high in the air, landing deep in left.

I channeled my anger into the baseball, and it paid off. Brandon didn't defeat me. He motivated me.

Brandon looked at me like I'd insulted his family. Next pitch, I drilled one right past him. First down the line. Then another to his left. He flinched.

Subconsciously, I was fucking with him.

I had dealt with hardcore street kids. This preppy, sheltered kid thought he could intimidate me. I didn't say a word. I just jogged back to my shortstop position like I had been doing my whole baseball life.

Coach and the batting practice pitcher were collecting baseballs scattered around the field. I set my glove down, wiped the sweat from my brow, and glanced up into the bleachers.

And that's when I saw her.

She was sitting near the top row, legs crossed, wearing bell-bottoms, sunglasses perched on her head like she didn't need them to see straight through you. Her hair was pulled back, hazel eyes catching the reflection of the sun.

She was about five-foot-six, slim, dirty-blonde hair. She wasn't clapping. She wasn't cheering. She was just watching. Watching the whole time.

I didn't know her name. Not yet. But something in her gaze made me stand up straighter. And for the first time in a long time, I didn't feel like a kid from the housing projects trying to prove something. I felt like someone worth watching.

Sonny spoke softly.

"That's the kind of moment that stays with you."

Jervin nodded.

"Not just the game. Not just the jersey. It was the feeling that maybe, just maybe, I wasn't invisible anymore.

She didn't say a word. Didn't wave. Just smiled. But that smile cracked something open. For the first time, I wasn't chasing the dream. I was being seen inside it."

The sun dipped low behind the bleachers, casting long shadows across the field. Jervin was taking grounders, focused and locked in. But Rafael, always observant, had noticed something else.

A girl.

Slim. Graceful. Dirty-blonde hair tied back. Her hazel eyes never left Jervin. She wasn't just watching tryouts. She was watching him.

Rafael, never shy, walked over casually. His steps were slow but respectful.

"Hi," he said.

The girl turned, a little startled by the sight of this large man.

"Hi," she replied, hesitantly.

Rafael smiled.

"That's my friend Jervin," he said. "I noticed you haven't taken your eyes off him."

She blushed, brushing a strand of hair behind her ear. "He's really good."

Rafael nodded.

"He's going to be a star."

She tilted her head.

"Where is he from?"

"The Lower East Side," Rafael said with quiet pride.

"Really?" she asked, surprised. Then she extended her hand.

"By the way, my name is Anna."

"Rafael," he said, gently shaking her hand. Her hands were feminine, her fingernails well manicured and tiny compared to Rafael's construction-worker hands.

"I'll introduce you to my friend after the tryouts," Rafael promised.

"You think he made the team?" Anna asked.

"If he didn't," Rafael said with a grin, "there should be an investigation."

Anna smiled. It wasn't polite. It was radiant. The kind of smile that hinted at something beginning.

From the field, Jervin glanced toward the bleachers and caught a glimpse of Rafael speaking to the mysterious girl. He didn't think much of it. Not yet. His focus stayed on the ball, the drills, the steady rhythm of proving himself.

But Rafael did.

He knew stories didn't always start on the field. Sometimes, they began in the stands.

Act 9: The Walk

The tryouts had ended, and the field was quiet now, just the soft rustle of leaves and the distant hum of life moving on. Jervin and Anna walked side by side down a tree-lined path near the park, the sky fading into a deep indigo.

"So, did you make the team?" Anna asked.

"Yes, I made the team. Coach said I'm his starting shortstop, and he plans on batting me second."

Jervin paused, then looked at Anna and smiled. "So, Anna… what's your last name?"

Anna smiled back, a hint of enthusiasm in her voice. "Johnson."

Jervin raised an eyebrow.

"Anna Johnson," he repeated playfully. "Where are you from?"

Anna hesitated for a moment, brushing a strand of hair from her face.

"The Upper East Side."

Jervin smirked.

"You sure there isn't going to be an APB out on you?"

Anna laughed, a light, melodic sound.

"Nooo," she said, nudging Jervin gently, almost childlike.

Jervin slowed his steps.

"So, Miss Johnson," he said with mock formality, "would you like to see a movie one night?"

"Sure, why not," she replied, her voice soft but certain.

"I heard *Saturday Night Fever* is good," Anna added.

Jervin squinted.

"Well, I guess I could survive two hours of disco."

"It's supposed to be good. John Travolta. Bee Gees music."

"Okay, don't twist my arm," Jervin said, grinning.

Anna laughed, then shifted the subject.

"I noticed you had a little male testosterone competition with Brandon."

"You know him?" Jervin asked, surprised.

"Well," Anna began, "I used to go out with him."

"You're kidding me," Jervin said, half in disbelief.

Anna laughed briefly, then turned serious. "No. Be careful with him. His father knows people, and he sits on the board. Try to have a good relationship with Brandon. You don't have to be his best friend, but remember, baseball is like music. You have to keep it in harmony so the rhythm works. Otherwise, it sounds like shit."

Jervin smirked.

"You're quite a philosopher. Was that Confucius?"

Anna smiled.

"Well, my family's into sports, and they always said team chemistry equals winning."

Jervin nodded. He took her point to heart.

A driver was waiting for Anna. She turned to him and asked, "You want a ride?"

Jervin hesitated, embarrassed about where he lived, and made an excuse.

"No, I'm good. I'm taking the subway."

"Okay. Good night," she said.

"Night," Jervin replied, waving as he walked away.

The walk turned into a revelation.

Act 10: Dinner with the Johnsons

Sonny leaned in, eyes wide.

"So, did you guys date?"

Jervin smiled, recalling the memory. "Yes. And after about a month, she invited me to dinner one evening. She asked me to dress formally, which I found strange, but I didn't question it. I threw on a blazer, dress shirt, slacks, and shoes, trying to look like I belonged somewhere important.

While I was getting ready, the phone rang. When I picked it up, it was Anna.

'A car is going to pick you up at six, so be ready.'

A car, I thought. Not a cab. Okay. I could live with that.

Around six, the driver arrived. We headed uptown. I figured she lived somewhere near East Harlem or close by. But then the driver stopped in front of this fancy building on the Upper East Side.

I asked, 'Why are we stopping?'

'We're here,' the driver said.

Dances with the Dirt

A man in a suit greeted me at the entrance. He looked like Mr. French from *Family Affair*, British accent and all.

'This way, sir,' he said.

Walking through the building, I thought this had to be a formal function. A ball. A gala. Something highbrow. But it wasn't. It was Anna's parents' apartment.

And this wasn't just another apartment. This place spelled wealth. Marble floors. Chandeliers. Art that looked like it had its own insurance policy.

Anna greeted me with a big smile. 'Hi,' she said, like it was just another casual Tuesday.

She introduced me to her parents. Her father shook my hand, firm and respectful. Her mother was warm and asked me about school. We ended up talking about New York cheesecake. I even made her laugh a couple of times.

During dinner, Mr. Johnson asked, 'So, what are your plans for the future?'

'I plan on going to college after high school,' I said."

"Aren't you a ballplayer?" he asked.

"Yes," I replied. "Even if I somehow get drafted, I'm going to decline and go to college. You never know I could break a leg, and it could be over."

Anna chimed in quickly. "Don't say that."

Mr. Johnson nodded. "He has a point. That's a good contingency plan. Smart and practical."

He looked at me differently after that. I wasn't just another frat-boy type like Brandon—guys Anna had brought home before with fake confidence and slick hair. He saw I was simple. Honest. No angle.

I felt overwhelmed, intimidated by their wealth. Marble floors. Chandeliers. Art that whispered insurance policies. But they made me feel comfortable. Up to a point.

Mrs. Johnson asked, "Jervin is an interesting name. Is that a family name?"

"Actually," I said, "I was named after both my grandfathers. My mother's father was named Jerry, and my father's father was named Vincenzo. He was from Sicily."

"And where is your mother from?" Mrs. Johnson asked.

I paused for a moment. "Puerto Rico."

A silence followed, as though a tribute were being paid. It wasn't rude… just awkward.

"I've heard it's a wonderful place," she finally said.

After dinner, Anna and I stepped outside.

"So, when were you going to tell me you were rich?" I asked.

Anna looked uneasy. Nervous. "Are you upset?"

"Fuck no," I said. "It's great. You have the world by the balls. I never had shit. This is different, I have to admit.

Unexpected and surreal, but… I could get used to it. I'm sure you've never smelled pee in the hallways."

She muffled a laugh.

"I really want to see where you live," she said.

"Why? It's the hood. Not much to see. Besides, it's dangerous. Your father would kill me if I brought you down there."

She didn't push. She just looked at me with those hazel eyes—curious, kind, and carrying a hint of fascination with the world I came from.

And I wondered if she was in love with me… or romanticizing where I was from.

Act 11: Knock on the Door

Sonny grinned. "So did Anna ever see your neighborhood? Where you lived?"

Jervin chuckled.

"Yeah. One day she showed up unannounced. It was a Saturday—I was lounging in sweatpants, half-watching a ball game, half dozing off. Then I heard a knock at the door. I thought it was my parents. They were off in Atlantic City and probably forgot their keys. We had a slam lock they could never figure out.

Anyway, I looked through the peephole—and it was Anna's driver. I was a little startled. I swear to God, the guy looked like a hitman. Black suit. Stone face. Posture like he'd just stepped out of a Scorsese flick.

I opened the door cautiously, just a crack. "What's going on?" I asked.

"Anna planned a surprise for you," said the driver—the man I jokingly called Mr. Fun.

I blinked. "Really?"

I opened the door wider and let him into the apartment. Trying to break the tension, I said, "You're not here to whack me, are you?"

He grinned. Barely. Like it hurt his face to smile.

"Okay," I said, "let me get out of these sweatpants and put on something nicer."

He nodded. "Do that."

I swear he tried to smile again—but it looked like it would've injured his cheekbones.

I threw on jeans, a clean shirt, and my best sneakers. Nothing fancy, but presentable.

I didn't know what the surprise was. But I knew one thing—Anna was stepping into my territory now. My world.

And part of me was nervous. Nervous because I was ashamed. Nervous because I didn't know how someone like her would see it.

The cracked walls. The hallways that smelled like bleach—and something worse. The elevators groaned like they had secrets.

Sonny leaned in, voice low and curious. "What was her reaction?"

Jervin smiled, eyes drifting back. "She was in the lobby, just standing there, taking it all in. The cracked tiles. The flickering lights. The smell of old radiator heat and fried food drifting from someone's apartment."

He paused, remembering.

"She looked around like she was in a museum."

I walked up to Anna. "Like my palace?" I asked.

She smiled. "It's different."

"What's your driver's name?" I asked. "We were never formally introduced."

"Marcus," she answered.

I nodded. "Tell Marcus there's a garage on Grand Street where he can park. We're going to walk. I want you to feel the hood."

She raised an eyebrow. "Walk?"

"Yeah, you know, that thing we do with our feet," I said sarcastically. "Listen, if you want a real tour, you have to earn it. No tinted windows. No bubble wrap."

I looked at her, testing her grit.

Marcus did not say much, just gave a nod and drove off. Probably relieved to be off duty for a bit. Taking orders from a rich teenager had to be challenging.

We stepped onto the sidewalk. The sun was low, casting long spring shadows across graffiti-tagged walls and corner bodegas. Kids played stickball in the street. A guy on the stoop nodded at me. I nodded back.

Anna walked beside me, her steps careful but curious. She did not flinch at the noise. She did not wrinkle her nose at the smells. She just observed.

"This is where I grew up," I said. "Where I learned to throw. How to duck. How to read people fast."

She looked around. "It's loud. But it's alive."

"Exactly," I said. "It's not pretty, but it's real."

Just as I said that, a tanned, Asian-looking kid came up to me.

"Yo, Jervin, what's up?" He hugged me.

"What's up, Chino? This is my friend Anna," I said.

Chino took a good look at Anna. "I see you're moving up in the world," he said, flashing his charm.

"Okay, fucking Romeo. You still doing throw-ups?"

"Yeah, I just finished one. I'll be doing more soon."

"Okay, Chino, we have to go. My girl here and I want to survey this beautiful land."

Chino laughed as we slapped hands.

Anna looked at me. "What's a throw-up?"

"Oh, that's a graffiti piece, like the ones we saw while walking, only his are nicer. Now if you want to see graffiti art, I want to show you a masterpiece."

"By the way," she asked curiously, "how do you know him?"

"Oh, we went to school together," I said as we walked.

"Is he Asian?"

I laughed. "No, he's Puerto Rican. We call him Chino because he looks Chinese."

"He's cute. That's interesting," Anna said.

"What's interesting?"

"That he looks Chinese and is a dark-skinned Puerto Rican."

"Oh, that's nothing," I said. "I have friends with blonde hair and blue eyes who speak better Spanish than me. We come in all flavors."

Anna laughed at that line, like she was etching it into her memory bank.

We passed the old candy store where I used to buy chocolate by the pound with change I found between the sofa cushions and my allowance.

We passed the barbershop I frequented as a child, where the guys argued about the Mets and the Yankees like it was a religion.

We passed the fire hydrant that turned into a summer fountain when the heat became unbearable. Finally, we arrived at Junior High School 56. And there it was. A masterpiece from the great graffiti artist known as Lee.

Anna stared at it.

"My God… that is beautiful. Did he do that with paint or a spray can?"

"Well, I remember he primed the wall, and the next day it was there. He did it all with a spray can," I said, recalling that day.

"That man is talented," Anna said in amazement.

"He did it when he was a teenager," I said.

"That's even more impressive," she replied.

Anna kept staring at the piece. Her eyes said everything. She was looking at the other side of town with wonder. She was starting to see me, not the ballplayer, not the dinner guest, but just Jervin from the Lower East Side.

Sonny said softly, "So it was like a sightseeing tour in real time for Anna. What did you do next?"

Jervin, reflective, voice steady.

"We started on Essex Street. She admired the cobblestones, said they looked like something from the nineteenth century. I told her I used to ride my bike down that street, but if you hit a bump, you were in trouble.

The street is paved now, but back in '78 it was cobblestone. Rough and real."

From a distance, the smell of vinegar and brine hit your senses. You could smell the pickles from two blocks away. In those days, the barrels were displayed right on the sidewalks.

Anna said, "I want to try one of those pickles."

"Okay," I said. "Let's go into Gus' Pickles."

Anna looked at the juicy pickle, took a bite, and pickle juice ran down her face. She started laughing.

"Oh my God, this is good."

The guy in the store smiled. I turned to him.

"Give me some extra napkins."

He nodded and handed me a stack.

Then I turned to Anna and, in a highbrow snob voice, said, "Tsk, tsk, dear. I can't take you to any establishment."

Anna and the guy behind the counter laughed.

Anna had a laugh that made you laugh too, but also made your heart flutter.

I was conflicted. I didn't know whether I liked her or if I was in love with her.

Our next stop was Chinatown. We had dim sum. Fried dumplings.

She loved it.

"I've never had food like this before," Anna said. "And these shrimp egg rolls are delicious."

Watching the delight on her face brought me joy. She wasn't just eating. She was experiencing the moment.

Our next stop was the World Trade Center.

"You know I've only been here once. On a class trip. Never on my own," Anna said.

"Well, now as a young lady, you are here," I told her.

I shared a story with her, a memory from when I was a kid.

"Me and my best friend Junior used to stand on Henry Street. We'd watch the sun reflect off the glass. It made the towers feel mythical. Like magic."

Anna smiled.

"I'm just visualizing you as a child," she said.

Our next stop was the Brooklyn Bridge. She wanted to walk into Brooklyn, a trip I had done dozens of times. It was her first.

She looked, smiled, and observed.

"I never realized how many people walk this bridge," she said.

"Thousands a day," I told her. "It's my favorite bridge."

We paused for a moment, watching the sun set. Suddenly, we kissed for what felt like an eternity. My heart pounded.

Then she shifted gears.

"I want to learn Spanish," she said enthusiastically.

I smiled.

"Okay, as long as you teach me French. You never know when you might need it."

After our brief time in Brooklyn, I told Anna, "Okay, let's head back. It's getting dark, and downtown Brooklyn is not that safe at night."

So we walked the bridge back into Manhattan and started toward Catherine Street.

Two young teens were arguing. One was Asian, the other Hispanic.

I put my hand on Anna's shoulder.

"Let's cross the street."

There was traffic, and as we waited for the light to change, we heard a bang.

We both turned. The Asian teen was standing over the other boy, gun in hand. The boy was bleeding on the pavement.

I froze. I put my hand over Anna's head and held her close.

"Don't scream," I whispered in her ear.

The teen stared at me, gun at his side.

Then suddenly, he took off running toward Chinatown.

"Should I call the police?" Anna asked, her voice shaking.

"No," I said. "Let's get out of here. This could be gang related."

Later, I heard through the grapevine that the teen who was shot had robbed the other boy's father. The shooter was a member of the notorious Ghost Shadows, a well organized criminal gang. My instincts were correct that night.

The boy died on his way to the hospital.

That day started with pickles and laughter. It ended with blood on the pavement.

Anna saw my world. All of it. The full force.

Act 12: The Aftermath

Sonny quietly asked,

"So, what happened afterward?"

Jervin's voice was low, reflective.

"After that, things changed. Not just between me and Anna, but inside me. That walk through the city, the laughter, the food, the bridge, and then the moment on Catherine Street, it was the full force in effect. Beauty and brutality side by side.

To her credit, Anna didn't run. She didn't flinch. Though shaken, she stayed. And that meant something.

We didn't talk on the ride home. Marcus drove in silence, and we followed suit. The laughter was gone, at least for the moment. Marcus knew. He had seen things in his day.

When we arrived at her building, she turned to me and said, 'I don't want this to be the last time we spend time in your world.'

'It's not a world, Anna. It's a maze. And you don't get to walk through it without scars.'

She nodded. She didn't argue. She held my hand a second longer than usual.

That night didn't end with a kiss. It ended with silence.

But it was the kind of silence that stays with you. The kind that signals you've changed."

Act 13: The Next Chapter

Sonny leaned in, voice low.

"So, what was the next chapter in your life?"

Jervin nodded.

"In 1980, my Ivy League high school made the city finals for the first time ever.

Unfortunately, we were obliterated by a high school team from the Bronx. Those kids were tough, real street ballers. Intimidating. My frat boy teammates weren't ready for that level of hunger.

I remember the Bronx team celebrating, Spanish music blasting, the girls singing along. It felt like a block party. Painful to watch."

Jervin paused.

"I saw Brandon sitting alone on the bench. Everyone else had already left. I walked over and sat next to him.

I said, 'Those kids schooled us today.'

Brandon stared straight ahead. Then out of nowhere, he blurted out, 'Those fucking spics.'

I turned and looked at him. I remembered what Anna had told me, and calmly said, 'You know, in two weeks when we graduate, I'm glad I'll never have to see your smug face again.'

I stood up, and as I walked away, I added, 'Good luck in life, bro.'

To my credit, I handled it without a physical confrontation. I could have punched Brandon, but Anna had warned me. I didn't take the bait.

As I walked away, I thought of Manny, and the irony that he was willing to die for this country, just so Brandon could insult me."

Act 14: The Conversation

Sonny, in a faint voice, asked, "Were you still dating Anna?"

Jervin paused for a moment and cleared his throat.

"Anna and I were still dating, but Marcus had to chaperone us everywhere. He was like a dark shadow. Anna's father didn't trust our relationship.

It was May 1980, a week before graduation. We were going to see *The Shining*. I kept imitating the creepy old lady's voice, and Anna laughed. Then she got serious.

'Jervin,' she said, 'I heard you received a scholarship to Miami University. Is that true?'

'Yes,' I said.

'Well, I think that's great,' she replied.

I was smiling, but then I paused.

'Wait. Where are you going to college?' I asked.

Anna couldn't meet my eyes.

'Harvard.'

Silence filled the air. Thick. Heavy.

Harry Albino

I broke it.

'So this means we won't be seeing each other anymore. Am I correct?'

She looked down, avoiding eye contact, until she finally gathered the courage to say what had to be said.

'Look, Jervin… I really like you. No, I love you. But my father has connections at Harvard. He's overprotective. He'll never let me go to Miami. He doesn't know anyone there. He doesn't think it's safe.'

I wasn't fully buying her explanation. I questioned her more directly.

'Is it because of the Cuban migration or immigration or whatever the fuck?' I asked, my voice louder now.

'That's part of it,' she said. 'But the other part is this. Harvard opens doors for me. Miami opens doors for you. Let's face it. No one scouts Ivy League schools for pro baseball. Miami is your best shot.'"

At the time, she had a point. But it also felt like she was trying to let me down gently. I felt her father could not picture me marrying his daughter. Or maybe she shared that same vision.

People with that kind of wealth and means do not marry down. They marry within their circle. Their class. Their comfort.

Later that night, life felt colder than usual. I kept thinking that love was not enough when the world had already drawn its lines.

Act 15: The Mirror

Sonny, in an even voice, said, "That kind of news changes everything."

Jervin nodded.

"It was only the beginning. As graduation approached, my father received a diagnosis. Hodgkin's lymphoma. He looked weak. I told my mother to focus on him and not worry about my ceremony.

I knew he was proud. But he was old school. You could not read him. Pride came in silence, not speeches."

So I gathered the closest members of my entourage. Rafael, of course.

Junior was still working at the sporting goods store. He had graduated the year before. I knew his big family would show up in full force. His little cousin Carolyn was a brat, but she was cute. She had a little girl crush on me, which I found adorable. I teased her like a big brother.

The final person I wanted at my graduation was George. It wouldn't be the same without him.

I had not seen George since eighth grade. So, I went back to my old junior high school to track him down.

Walking through those doors felt surreal. The same cracked linoleum. The same smell of cafeteria pizza and pencil shavings. Somehow the school looked smaller. Or maybe I had just gotten bigger. My steps echoed louder.

And there was the same security guard. Overweight. Lazy. Still parked behind the desk like a statue.

"Can I help you?" he asked, barely looking up.

I could not help thinking, how could this guy catch any of these kids? The only thing he could catch was a cold. His thighs rubbed together like two stumps ready to start a forest fire.

"I'm looking for George," I said.

"George who?" he asked, in a slow, syrupy tone.

"George Weinstein," I replied, trying not to show my annoyance.

"Oh. That George. He doesn't work here anymore. Graduated law school."

"Really?" I said, surprised. "Do you know where he's practicing?"

He paused and looked at me more closely.

"Who are you?" he asked.

"Jervin. Jervin Class. I used to be a student here."

His eyes lit up.

"Wait. You're that kid from the newspaper. Got a scholarship to a Florida college?"

"Yeah. Miami University," I said, slightly annoyed.

"It wasn't front page, but it was in the sports section," he added, almost proudly.

"About George. Do you know where he's practicing?"

"Actually," he said, reaching into a drawer, "he left his business card. Gave one to each staff member before he resigned. Here. Write down the information."

He handed me the card along with a piece of paper and a pen. I scribbled down the details, folded the paper, and slipped it into my pocket.

"Thank you," I said.

He nodded. As I turned to leave, he called out, "Good luck, kid."

I smiled. And I felt bad for what I had been thinking. I had been channeling my thirteen year old self, judging him through the lens of a kid who didn't know any better.

But I wasn't a kid anymore.

I had come looking for George.

Instead, I found a mirror.

Act 16: To George

Sonny leaned back, eyes narrowing with interest. "You went looking for George? That must have been something."

Jervin nodded, a slow smile tugging at the corner of his mouth.

"George's office was on 40th and Madison. I figured I'd take the F train, get off at 42nd Street, Bryant Park. Today, that park is a gem. Back in 1980, it was seedy. Especially after dark.

I walked toward Madison Avenue. Passed a Chock Full o' Nuts and a Blarney Stone. The city smelled like hot pretzels and exhaust. I liked it that way.

I finally reached the building. Got on the elevator and pressed the button for the seventh floor. Other people were in there with me. I hated being in elevators with strangers. The awkward silence. Everyone pretending not to exist. Each floor ticked by like a countdown to something I couldn't name."

Seventh floor. Thank God.

The doors opened with a tired groan. I stepped into a hallway lined with frosted glass and the low hum of typewriters behind closed doors. The carpet was a dull gray, worn thin down the middle like a path carved by years of pacing.

Suite 714.

I knocked once.

"Come in," a voice called out.

There she was. A secretary in a sharp gray suit, sitting behind a mahogany desk. Behind her, a wall lined with framed degrees and photos of George with Little League teams. I spotted one with me in it.

She looked to be in her thirties. Attractive. Glasses perched just right.

"Good morning, ma'am," I said.

She smiled. "Can I help you?"

"I'm here to see Mr. Weinstein."

"Do you have an appointment?"

"No, but George will be happy to see me."

She nodded toward the waiting area. "Have a seat."

As I sat down, she asked, "Sir, what is your name?"

"Tell Mr. Weinstein it's Jervin Class."

I waited. I could hear George's voice in the back. It sounded like he was wrapping up with a client.

Then he turned the corner, did a double take, and realized it was me.

"Jervin," he said. His eyes lit up.

"I came by, George, to see how you're doing. And to tell you I'm graduating. I want you to be there. I'm heading to Miami University in the fall."

George smiled and nodded. I saw it on his face. That look. Like a proud father.

"And George, if by some chance I make it to the next level, I might need your help."

"Of course, Jervin. Anything you need, you can count on me."

"Can you attend my graduation, George? It would mean the world to me."

"Where and when?"

"Thursday. Nine a.m. Madison Square Garden."

"I'll be there."

George extended his hand.

But I hugged him instead.

He felt emotional. I could tell by the way he held on. There was a slight catch in his voice when he said, "You've grown. How tall are you now?"

"Six feet. One sixty."

"You're not the quiet kid in the field anymore."

"No," I said. "But I still remember how to dance with the dirt."

As I was leaving, George turned to his secretary.

"Helen, this is the kid I was telling you about."

Helen looked at me, then smiled. It was a pretty smile, but a serious one. Not forced, but not entirely warm.

Maybe she was upset because I called her ma'am. Maybe I had aged her in a way she didn't appreciate. Or maybe she was just trying to figure out what kind of kid could leave that kind of mark on George Weinstein.

Either way, I did not care.

I was not there to impress her.

I was there to say thank you.

To George.

Act 17: Graduation Day

Thursday. 9 a.m. Madison Square Garden.

The air was thick with June heat and nerves. Families poured in from every borough. Mothers in pantsuits. Fathers in pressed suits. Cousins with disposable cameras. Little brothers in clip on ties. The smell of cologne, hairspray, and ambition filled the arena.

I stood backstage in my cap and gown, fingers twitching, heart pounding. I wasn't nervous about walking. I was nervous about who would be watching.

I peeked through the curtain.

There they were.

Rafael, standing tall in a crisp navy blue suit, arms crossed, eyes scanning the stage like a coach before a game.

Junior, grinning wide, surrounded by his loud, loving family, sneaking sunflower seeds. His little cousin Carolyn waved a homemade sign that read, "Go Jervin!" in glitter.

George, in a navy blazer, tie straight this time. He nodded at me like we had just closed a deal.

Then I saw my mother. I was surprised. She looked tired, worn from caring for my father, but in my eyes she was glowing.

My father could not make it. He was too weak. But I knew he was proud. I imagined him in his recliner, remote in hand, pretending to flip channels while watching the clock.

The ceremony blurred. Names called. Tassels turned. Applause rising and falling like waves.

When they called mine, "Jervin Class, Miami University, full athletic scholarship," the crowd erupted.

I heard Rafael's whistle. Junior's shout. Little Carolyn screaming, "Jervin, Jervin," until Junior hushed her. Laughter rippled through the crowd. She was not embarrassed. She just smiled. I smiled back at her.

I walked across the stage like it was a bridge between two worlds.

Afterward, in the chaos of hugs and photos, George pulled me aside.

"You did it," he said.

"We did it," I replied.

He smiled. "You ready for Miami?"

"Yeah," I said. "But I'll never forget where I'm from."

Act 18: Anna

Sonny raised his eyebrows, a knowing smile tugging at the corner of his mouth.

"Did you see Anna that day?"

Jervin grinned, brushing imaginary lint off his lapel.

"Yeah. I spotted her and walked toward her, a big grin on my face."

She was standing near the far side of the arena, just outside the crowd, wearing a cream colored dress and a navy blazer. Her hair was pinned back, elegant. She looked like she belonged in a Kennedy photo. Poised. Polished. Untouchable.

"You, my love, look gorgeous as ever," I told her.

Anna tilted her head, that radiant smile blooming. "And you look so handsome. That suit makes you look powerful." She started fixing my tie.

I chuckled, easing the tension. "I was thinking of wearing a bow tie, but I would look like a waiter in a Mexican restaurant."

Anna laughed. The kind of laugh that makes you feel like the world is all right.

"You are ridiculous," she said.

We stood outside Madison Square Garden. The crowd was thinning, the city humming in the background. The air was warm, but not heavy. The kind of afternoon that promises something.

Anna stood beside me, her eyes scanning the street, then settling on mine.

"What are your plans afterward?" she asked softly.

I shrugged. "I was thinking Katz's with my entourage. Pastrami on rye with mustard. And of course, a juicy pickle."

She stepped closer, lowering her voice.

"No, Jervin. I mean after that."

My heart skipped.

I didn't know if she meant this summer, this fall, or the rest of my life.

"Do you mean… meet up?" I finally blurted out.

Anna's eyes locked with mine. Something flickered there. Something tender. Something final.

Her voice dropped into something private, like a secret meant only for me.

"Yes. I have a parting gift for you," she said.

I didn't know if she meant a kiss, a letter, or something that could change everything.

But I knew one thing.

She wasn't just saying goodbye.

She was leaving a mark.

Act 19: Brandon

Sonny leaned forward, curiosity flickering in his eyes.
"Before you get to the next story, I'm just curious. Whatever happened to that third baseman? Brandon, the bully?"

Jervin smirked.

"Brandon…"

He let the name hang in the air like a nauseating smell.

"Well, from what I found out, he went to an Ivy League college. Graduated. Went into politics. His family was well connected. The kind of Christmas card from a senator connected."

Sonny raised an eyebrow.

"But then," Jervin continued, "he got himself into trouble. Real trouble. Indicted and convicted. Sentenced to federal prison. Fraud, bribery. Your typical political starter pack."

Sonny let out a low whistle.

"But here's the kicker," Jervin said, leaning back. "His family pulled strings. Made calls. Who knows what else? And the president issued him a pardon."

Sonny blinked. "You're kidding."

Jervin shook his head. "Nope. Brandon walked out of prison like it was a country club. Probably had a driver waiting."

He paused, then added with a shrug, "Privileged people get second chances handed to them. Others have to fight for every inch.

Receiving a pardon after a felony conviction doesn't necessarily ruin a political career. If anything, these days it can look like a badge of honor."

Act 20: The Hotel on Houston Street

Sonny leaned in, voice curious but gentle. "So did you see Anna that night?"

Jervin answered without hesitation, like the memory had happened yesterday.

"After dinner with Rafael, Junior, George, and my mother, I met Anna."

He paused, something flickering behind his eyes.

"Well, technically Marcus picked me up on Houston Street. The car was sleek, polished, quiet inside. Like it carried secrets."

He smiled.

"Anna was still in her graduation outfit. She looked elegant, with a shimmer that caught the streetlights. Like a dream that hadn't faded away.

"So," I asked, settling into the seat beside her, "where are we going?"

"You'll see," she said, eyes forward.

Marcus drove in silence, like always. We passed a familiar corner, an old bodega, the ghost of stickball games and fire hydrant summers. The city blurred past like a memory on fast forward.

Then he pulled up in front of a hotel. One of those places with gold trim and a door attendant who didn't blink.

"Come on," she said, stepping out of the car.

I followed.

No questions. Just trust.

She leaned into the car window. "Be back in three hours."

Marcus nodded. No expression. Just protocol.

I hesitated. "Are you sure you want to do this, Anna?"

"Yes," she said, without flinching.

"One question," I added, half joking. "Is Marcus going to kill me, chop me up, and feed me to his pit bull?"

She gave me a dry look. "He hasn't mentioned it yet."

I laughed. A quick, nervous laugh.

"No, silly," she said, her voice softening. "In fact, for the first time in his life, he's going to look the other way."

We stepped into the lobby.

Marble floors gleamed like they had never seen dirt. Crystal chandeliers hung like frozen fireworks. The air smelled like polished wood and quiet money.

But Anna's hand in mine made it feel like home.

"I want you to remember, Jervin," she said. "And I want you to remember me, no matter what happens in life."

I didn't answer right away.

I didn't know what waited behind those closed doors. But I knew one thing. I wasn't the same kid who once watched her from the bleachers.

I had grown. Not just taller. Not just stronger. But sharper. Quieter. More aware of what things cost.

Later, Sonny asked, "Was Marcus really that scary?"

Jervin smiled.

"Yeah. He looked like he could've been cast on The Sopranos. Big guy. Stone face. Like he had a shovel in the trunk and a story ready for the police."

Sonny laughed.

"But he knew one thing," I said. "He understood that I loved Anna. That I'd never hurt her."

I paused, then added, "Besides, he worked for Anna's father. And he took orders from a rich teenager."

Jervin shook his head, still smiling.

"Now that is something."

Act 21: The Wedding That Wasn't

Sonny chuckled, shaking his head. "I'm telling you, this sounds like a novella on Telemundo."

Jervin slipped into an exaggerated Spanish accent. "Esta noche, en La Boda Que Nunca Fue…"

They both laughed.

"We approached the hotel clerk," Jervin continued. "He was an older Jewish guy, wearing a yarmulke, maybe fifty. He looked us up and down. Gave us the once over. Skeptical."

Sonny grinned. "Like he was trying to figure out if you were guests or grifters."

"Exactly," Jervin said. "I was in a suit that wasn't necessarily an Armani. Anna looked like a Vogue cover. We did not match. Not on paper. Not in person."

"What'd he say?" Sonny asked.

Jervin smirked. "Nothing at first. Just raised an eyebrow like he was waiting for us to explain ourselves."

The clerk kept his head down. When he realized we weren't leaving, he looked up.

"How are you kids?"

I didn't flinch.

I picked Anna up in my arms, half joking, half serious, and said, "She is my lovely bride, and we are here to celebrate our wedding day."

The clerk raised an eyebrow. "I don't see rings."

Anna, cool as ever, reached into her handbag and pulled out five crisp hundred dollar bills. She slid them across the counter like playing cards.

"Rings?" she said. "We bring receipts."

The clerk blinked.

"Rings? What rings?" he replied, suddenly cooperative, as he took the money and slid us a key.

Act 22: The Best Night

Dances with the Dirt

We rode the elevator in silence, the kind that hums with anticipation.

The room had soft lighting, pristine sheets, and a view of the city that felt like it was holding its breath.

It was a beautiful moment. Being intimate with the woman you love, yet knowing deep down it would soon become a memory.

Later, as we were dressing, I looked at Anna and said, "I feel like a trick," half laughing, half hurting.

She laughed, catching the street slang instantly. "I'm paying for your services," she teased, still laughing.

But I knew it wasn't about money with her. It was about self worth.

And for once, I didn't feel cheap.

She made me feel chosen.

As I buttoned my shirt, grinning, I joked, "Damn, my hair looks like shit. You are an animal."

She walked over, placed her hand on my chest, and caressed it. Then she kissed me. It wasn't a rushed kiss.

It was the kind of kiss that said, "I see you. I chose you."

My heart was pounding, not just from the kiss, but from everything.

And for two minutes, the world stopped pretending.

That was the best night of my young life.

Nothing could've topped it.

Even my high school diploma felt secondary.

Act 23: The Last Summer

Sonny asked softly, "So did you see each other again that summer?"

Jervin smiled, eyes distant.

"The first place I took her one summer afternoon was a wall on the Lower East Side."

We stood there, just the two of us, staring at it.

Anna ran her fingers across the paint, then stepped back.

It was a throw up by Chino. Big, bold letters: RIP Manny, with a mural of Manny's face, eyes soft, smile frozen in time. Signed C2.

"It's beautiful," Anna said.

"It is," I replied. "Chino knew Manny. This was his tribute."

We didn't speak after that. There are moments that don't need words.

Later, Marcus drove us to Coney Island. We stopped to admire the Warriors painting, the one used in the movie. It felt like we were witnessing history, not just watching it.

I remember the boardwalk.

She kicked off her shoes and walked barefoot, her toes brushing the worn wood. The air smelled like salt and sugar, cotton candy, sea spray, and fried dough.

We joked around, laughing like kids.

Her laughter echoed louder than the roller coasters.

We went to Nathan's.

I told her, "There are no Nathan's hot dogs at Harvard."

She just smiled, that knowing smile, even with mustard in the corner of her mouth.

I wiped it away with a napkin.

Next, I talked her into riding the roller coaster and the Hell Hole. She screamed, then laughed hysterically. It was hilarious watching Marcus ride with us, stone faced, arms crossed, like he was on the M15 bus.

"My heart almost dropped!" she said, clutching my arm like I was her anchor.

A song started playing from a nearby boom box, bouncing across the boardwalk.

"What's the name of that song? I keep hearing it," she asked.

"It's Kurtis Blow. The Breaks," I said.

"I like it. The sound is cheerful and uplifting," she said.

"Yeah," I grinned. "And he does Bar Mitzvahs."

She let out a laugh, loud, real, unfiltered.

Act 24: Strawberry Fields

Afterward, we went to Strawberry Fields.

We lay on the grass, holding hands, watching the clouds drift like slow moving dreams.

"Imagine," Anna said softly. "John Lennon lives here."

She turned to me and gave me her smile.

The one that always melted my heart.

Act 25: The Goodbye

Then the day came.

The one we hadn't wanted to name. The one that felt like a page turning before the ink was dry.

Anna and Marcus drove me to the airport. Bags packed. My stomach churning—a feeling in my chest like

I'd never felt before. Like excitement and heartbreak were dancing together.

We pulled up to LaGuardia.

I looked at her, tried to keep it together.

"So," I said, "I guess this is it."

Anna leaned in, fighting back tears, and whispered in my ear, "You are going to be a star."

Then she kissed me.

Not rushed. Not dramatic.

Just real.

Marcus stepped forward and shook my hand. Firm. Respectful.

"Take care of her," I told him.

He nodded. No words. Just a gesture that said, *I see you.*

And then I was off.

Miami-bound.

Sonny wiped his eye, pretending it was dust.

"That kind of goodbye… it stays with you."

Jervin nodded.

He was silent for close to half a minute.

Sonny didn't push. He just waited.

Because memories don't need words.

They need space.

Act 26: The Warm-Up

Sonny leaned back, changing the mood.

"So, let's talk about Miami."

Jervin's tone shifted, lighter now. More upbeat.

"I arrived in Miami a couple of weeks before classes started. I needed time to get situated, to breathe in the new air and figure out how the city moved."

He smiled, remembering.

"I fell in love fast. South Beach felt like Greenwich Village with a beach—artsy, electric—but with palm trees and an ocean breeze. And with a twist of Columbus Circle. Fancy, but not fake."

He paused, eyes distant.

"The water was blue. Real blue. The sand was the color it was supposed to be—not gray. Not littered. No dead jellyfish. No seaweed tangling your ankles."

He laughed softly.

"Miami Beach reminded me of a beach in Puerto Rico called Cana Gorda. Fat Sugarcane. Dune sand, soft, warm, and blue."

Jervin nodded, as if confirming it to himself.

"Miami Beach—I loved it."

I wandered into Cuban restaurants that reminded me of home.

The smell of garlic and pork. The clatter of dominoes. The rhythm of Spanish music bouncing off the walls.

It felt like New York—but with sunlight.

I asked one of the restaurant owners if he was hiring part-time. He looked me up and down, sizing me up. Impressed by how I spoke English and Spanish fluently—and how I carried myself.

Anna's etiquette lessons—unintended—worked.

She was a good influence.

More than she realized.

Then came the surprise:

Junior started sending me money orders every month.

I figured business must be booming at Jerry's Sporting Goods Store.

That gesture? It meant everything to me.

Authentic loyalty like that doesn't come often.

It wasn't just cash—it was a reminder that someone back home believed in me. That someone remembered me.

I had six months to train before I'd take the diamond with my new team.

I wanted to be ready.

Sonny asked, "So what did you do to prepare yourself?"

Jervin leaned back, a small smile forming.

"One day, I was flipping through a magazine and saw this fifty-year-old man with a well-defined physique. I read about his routine."

Sonny raised an eyebrow. "Which was?"

"One hundred push-ups a day. One hundred pull-ups a day. One hundred dips a day. Weights once a week. Jog two miles a day."

Sonny let out a whistle. "That's kind of a tall order."

Jervin grinned, pride in his voice. "Sonny, I was eighteen years old—with energy for days. That was a cakewalk for me. I had no unhealthy habits and ate well. The routine was simple. Brutal, but effective."

He paused, eyes narrowing with memory.

"So I started quietly. No fanfare. Just sweat and repetition. Because spring was coming, and I wasn't just training for baseball."

He looked at Sonny.

"I was training for everything. Every drop of sweat was a promise—to me, to Rafael, to Junior, to Anna, to my parents. Even to George."

Jervin's voice softened.

"I wasn't just building muscle. I was building belief."

Sonny chuckled, shaking his head.

"You didn't just warm up. You lit the fuse."

Act 27: Back Home

Sonny leaned in. "What was your next move?"

Jervin exhaled, a wry smile forming. "Miami had been warm. I got spoiled. But New York in December hit differently. The cold bit through my jacket, but the city felt like home—gritty, loud, familiar."

Sonny grinned. "So, you had a reverse culture shock?"

Jervin laughed. "You could say that."

He paused, then continued.

"I tried to acclimate to the unfamiliar. My classmates in Florida talked about things that didn't register—beach parties, boat culture, high school rivalries I'd never heard of."

He shook his head, smiling at the memory.

"I engaged with the young ladies on campus, but they weren't like Anna. I mean, they were nice. But I didn't have the same connection with any of them."

He looked down for a beat.

"Anna had set the bar so high, I couldn't pretend to lower it."

Sonny nodded slowly. "I get that. It's hard to lower the bar when it's set so high. It's like you drive a Porsche, then you downgrade to a Toyota."

Jervin smirked, but it faded quickly.

"Anyway, a couple of days before Christmas, I flew back to New York. One of the first things I did was call Anna's home, hoping we could meet up for the holidays."

The phone rang.

Mr. Johnson answered.

"How you doing, Mr. Johnson? This is Jervin. Is Anna back from college?"

There was a pause.

"No, Jervin. I'm sorry. She's not going to be back for the holidays. She's spending it at Harvard."

I felt a pang of disappointment. But then he continued.

"Jervin, you're a nice kid, but Anna is moving on with her life. She's studying to be a lawyer, and she has a place near Harvard. She's going to stay there for the duration of her studies. I suggest you forget about her and just move on with your life. I'm sure you'll find somebody nice."

I was stunned.

Didn't know what to say.

My heart dropped. I remember my pulse beating fast.

All I could blurt out was, "Thank you."

And I hung up the phone.

It was as if someone had just told me someone died.

Sonny sat back quietly. "Wow."

Jervin's voice dropped.

"I'd been thinking on the flight that we'd meet up, spark those magical moments again. I'd built a holiday around hope. And when it vanished… it felt like the whole season vanished."

Sonny leaned in, his voice barely above a whisper. "What'd you do?"

Jervin's voice stayed low.

"I calmly got dressed. I told my parents I was going for a walk. My face was ashen, my heart broken."

He paused, eyes clouded with memory.

"I walked to a park and made sure it was empty. The cold didn't matter. It couldn't touch what I was feeling."

He looked down.

"I sat on a bench and put my head in my hands—and for the first time I could remember, I cried."

He let the silence breathe.

"It was a painful cry. The kind that hurts your guts. And when it's done, you feel hollow. Like something's been scooped out of you."

He exhaled slowly.

"I gathered myself. Wiped my face. And decided to visit Junior.

I headed to Jerry's Sporting Goods."

Junior was wrapping up his shift when he spotted me.

"Jervin," he said, pulling me into a hug.

After the debacle with Anna, Junior brought a little joy back into my chest.

"Have you seen Rafael?" I asked.

"He went to the Dominican Republic to be with his family," Junior said, wiping down the counter. "Give me a few minutes, Jervin."

"Need a ride home?" he asked.

"I'm only a few blocks away," I said. "But okay. I want to see your new ride."

When he finished, we walked outside.

There it was—a 1980 used Trans Am. Black, sleek, and loud even when parked. It looked like freedom.

But freedom with a price tag.

"You must've saved a long time to buy this," I said, eyeing the chrome.

"Yeah," Junior said. "I had to get a loan. But it was worth it."

I didn't think much of it. Just nodded.

"Thanks for the money orders, Junior. You know I'll pay you back one day."

"Don't worry about it, mi hermano," he said, placing a hand on my shoulder.

That's when I noticed—Junior stood out. Designer shirt. Fancy sneakers. Sharper than usual. Then we boarded the Trans Am.

"So… did you hear from Anna?" Junior asked.

It was a question I'd been trying to avoid.

I tried to play it cool. I didn't want to show the hurt.

"She's spending the holidays at Harvard," I said, keeping my voice even.

Junior paused. "Really?" he said, like he wasn't buying it.

Then, after a beat, he blurted out the obvious. "Don't take this the wrong way, Jervin. But I think you should move on."

The thought infuriated me.

"Move on? From what—magic? From the only woman who ever made me feel like more than a zip code?"

Junior stayed quiet. He let me vent.

He knew I was hurting. And that's what friends do.

They listen.

After about a minute of silence, Junior turned on the radio. It was loud at first, but he turned it down.

Teena Marie was playing—*Beyond the Groove.*

Then Junior broke the silence.

"You know she's white."

I smiled for a minute.

Junior had a way of making me laugh, even when life felt like shit.

He was there when Manny died. So was Rafael.

At that moment, I wished Rafael were around. He'd become like my big brother. He understood women better than Junior ever could.

Finally, we pulled up to my building.

We did our homeboy handshake.

I stepped out.

"Yo, Jervin!" Junior yelled.

I turned around.

"Mi hermano," he said, thumping his chest with his fist.

I nodded and walked away.

I was sulking inside, but like Rafael once told me, it's a feeling. You'll get over it.

As I stood in the lobby for a minute, I looked through the scratched plexiglass.

I saw Junior laughing with a group of guys older than him.

They looked like the kind of men who didn't laugh unless something was burning.

And I wondered if I had come home to a place that no longer knew me.

Sonny exhaled slowly.

"Sometimes coming home feels like leaving all over again."

Act 28: Dance with the Dirt

"Let's talk about your first practice," Sonny said, leaning forward.

Jervin smiled. "Spring arrived like a promise."

"My big day was ahead—first practice with my college team. The scholarship guaranteed me a spot, but not a starting position. That had to be earned.

"I stepped onto the field, and for a moment, it felt like Little League all over again."

He paused.

"But it wasn't. This was another level. Faster-paced. Real stakes."

"I stood at shortstop, nerves buzzing. Rafael's voice echoed in my head: *Dance with the dirt.*"

"Grounders came fast. I moved with rhythm, not panic."

"The coach watched, arms crossed."

"'Good footwork, kid,' he said. 'It's like you're dancing out there.'"

"'I have music in my head, Coach,' I replied."

Coach gave me a half-smile. The kind that says, *I like your edge—but don't push it.*

Sonny laughed. "By the way, in case people weren't aware—Jervin brought a journal with him. He's actually reading excerpts from it."

He looked at the camera.

"But the rest? That comes from the heart."

"Next came batting practice."

George's voice echoed in my head.

Think middle. Go with the pitch. Don't pull everything. Don't lean. Elbows up. Keep your weight back. Don't open your hips too soon. Keep your eyes on the ball.

I stepped to the plate, locked in.

Line drives. Opposite-field hits. Even a couple of home runs.

No one was ever going to call me a Punch and Judy hitter again, I thought to myself. I was finding my rhythm. My confidence. My place.

Then ten days later, everything paused.

There was an assassination attempt on President Reagan in Washington, D.C.

The nation held its collective breath. Classes stopped. Radios buzzed. TVs flickered with breaking news. Even on the field, the crack of the bat gave way to silence.

For Jervin, it was a jarring reminder: no matter how fast you run, the world can still stop you in your tracks.

Sonny leaned in. "What were your thoughts on Reagan being shot?"

Jervin exhaled. "I wasn't sure. He was an older man, but strong. I saw it on TV. I couldn't even tell he'd been shot."

He paused.

"In moments like that, you want to hear a voice that makes you feel comfortable. I contemplated calling Anna… but I could hear Mr. Johnson's voice in my head: *Move on.*"

He looked down, then back up.

"That same day, a couple of letters arrived from Junior and Rafael. They weren't just letters. Each one had a money order inside. A hundred dollars each."

"In 1981, two hundred dollars was money you could live on for a couple of weeks. It helped me buy schoolbooks, food, and essentials. It spared me from having to work. I already had my hands full—with practice, class, and my workout routine."

He leaned back, eyes distant.

"That night, March 30, 1981, I was in my dorm room. Leaning against the wall, near the window. The moonlight was beaming, adding extra light."

"I sat with the letters in my hand. Ink still fresh. Paper still warm."

"It wasn't just a journey."

"It was belief."

"And when you're far from home... belief is everything."

Sonny nodded slowly, his voice soft.

"You weren't just ready for the season."

He looked at Jervin.

"You were ready for life."

Act 29: The Fifth Game

"Did you start great in college baseball?" Sonny asked.

Jervin cleared his throat.

"Well... after that ten-day delay, it was showtime. I had built it all up in my head—the moment I would shine, prove myself, silence the doubts."

He paused.

"But the first four games? Brutal."

"I looked lost at the plate. Seven strikeouts. Zero for eighteen."

"Damn," Sonny muttered.

"My swing felt heavy. My timing was off. Teammates gave me that look—the kind that says he's overrated."

"I felt it. I felt them."

"I started thinking about quitting. Packing it up. Heading back to New York."

"At least there, I knew the streets."

"Here? I felt like a ghost."

"No Anna. No Rafael. No Junior."

"Just silence."

"There had to be a turning point," Sonny said. "Otherwise, you wouldn't be here."

Jervin nodded. "Yeah. Game Five was coming. And for the first time—I wasn't scared."

"I was hungry."

"A couple of days before the game, Coach pulled me aside. Put his hand on my shoulder, looked me straight in the eye. His voice was calm, but firm."

"'You know who Willie Mays is?' he asked."

"'Of course,' I said."

"'When he first got called up, he was hitless in his first twelve at-bats. Seven strikeouts. He even asked to be sent back to the minors.'"

I blinked. "'So what happened?' I asked."

"'Leo Durocher told him no. You know why?' Coach said."

"'Why?'"

"'Because he believed in the Say Hey Kid,' Coach said, steady."

Then he looked me dead in the eyes. His blue eyes locked into mine.

"'Kid, I believe in you. There's a reason college recruiters came to your high school. You weren't handed a scholarship because you're some rich guy's kid. You earned it. Every swing. Every sprint. Every damn blister.'"

He paused, then smiled.

"'Relax. Have fun. Enjoy the game. You're not performing open-heart surgery—you're playing baseball. If you strike out, no one's going to die.'"

I laughed. I couldn't help it. The analogy was ridiculous to an eighteen—soon-to-be-nineteen—year-old.

I didn't know if I'd hit a ball in the next game.

But I knew I wasn't quitting.

His words started to settle.

And for the first time in weeks, I felt something.

Not in my swing.

In my spirit.

Sonny leaned forward, eyes gleaming.

"That's the kind of story that makes you want to lace up again."

Act 30: The Turnaround

"So, you had this resurgence," Sonny said. "What happened next?"

Jervin leaned back, a grin tugging at the corner of his mouth.

"After the heart-to-heart with Coach, something clicked."

"First came the singles. Then more. Then a couple of doubles."

"One game—three hits, two RBIs, three stolen bases."

"And finally—the power started to show."

"RBIs started piling up like loose change in a dugout cup."

"And the dugout? It finally felt like home."

Sonny raised an eyebrow. "So, was this a mechanical thing?"

Jervin nodded. "The truth? I adjusted my stance. Worked on some upgrades with the batting instructor. And I switched from a 33-ounce bat to a 32-ounce bat."

He smiled.

"That one ounce made a world of difference—quicker hands, better bat control, more whip."

"The victories started rolling in."

"And funny how winning changes everything."

"Teammates who barely nodded before now slapped my back. The 'overrated' whispers faded. I wasn't just part of the team—I was helping lead it."

"And in every clubhouse or locker room, there's always a comedian."

"Locker room talk. Not for the sensitive."

Sonny chuckled. "This is so true. I can attest to that from experience."

Jervin grinned. "One day, Rico launched into his routine."

"'Yo, I was watching *Gilligan's Island* the other day. Yo, what's up with Gilligan? Always chasing the fat ass, Skipper. I mean, you've got Mary Ann and Ginger. I'd be fucking both of them.'"

The guys started laughing.

"'Yo, even Mrs. Howell would be in trouble.'"

More laughter.

"'I'd hit that ass so good, she'd leave Thurston. I'd be like, "Yo, Thurston, I done tore that ass up. Lovey ain't coming back. Yo, she in my hut, son."'"

The room erupted.

It was crude. Wild. Hilarious.

But that's how it was.

No filter. Just guys blowing off steam and talking shit.

We were riding the height of a winning streak.

"I can tell you—when teams bond like that, the chemistry grows," Sonny said. "And sometimes, that turns into winning."

"Absolutely," Jervin replied.

"Miami University was electric. The program was strong. The sun was constant."

"The rhythm of the city matched the rhythm of the game."

"The city moved like my bat—loose, fast, full of heat."

"And slowly, New York started to fade."

"Not disappear. Just… soften."

"I was building something new."

"And for the first time, I wasn't just hoping."

"I was believing."

"In the game. In the team. In myself."

Sonny leaned back, nodding.

"From ghost to leader. That's a hell of a turnaround."

Act 31: Clearing Out

"So, what happened next?" Sonny asked.

Jervin's eyes lit up.

"It was the best spring of my young life."

"Just like my senior year of high school, my team made it to the College World Series final."

"I'd be lying if I told you it wasn't exciting."

"There was a camera crew filming the game. Scouts in the stands. For the first time, the nation was about to get a look at who Jervin Class really was."

"The stakes were higher."

"The crowd louder."

"The pressure heavier."

"So how did you do?" Sonny asked.

Jervin smiled, eyes flickering with memory.

"I played a solid tournament. Good numbers. Clutch moments."

He paused.

"Like a game-winning walk-off home run in the first game."

"That was thrilling. I'd never done that before."

"I felt like I was floating as I rounded the bases."

"The crowd noise was like a loud murmur—blurred, distant, but alive."

"'You're a legend!' Rico yelled."

I just smiled.

"'Legends don't fan seven times in four games,' I said, half-joking."

"But they can rise like the Phoenix," I added, sounding like a fortune-cookie philosopher.

Sonny grinned. "That must've been the thrill of your life."

"Yes, it was," I said. "And then, in the championship game… we fell short."

"Again, I was on the losing end of a big game."

"The last out was a weak, easy pop-up to the second baseman. And as it dropped into his glove, so did our dreams."

"It was silence for us."

"Again—a bridesmaid."

"In the locker room, Coach gave us a speech. You know… that speech."

"'You guys can be proud. You had a terrific season. You have nothing to be ashamed of. No matter what—when this experience, or experiment, or whatever you want to call it—is over, you will come out on top.'"

"I'll be honest—I didn't know if I believed him."

"But I knew I had given everything."

"And sometimes, that has to be enough."

"But my goal has always been to win."

"The guys in the locker room nodded. A couple stared at the floor like it owed them something. A few wiped away tears."

"After the speech, no one spoke."

"Cleats scraped the concrete."

"I turned to my locker. Cleaned it out—glove, bat, cleats, and all the other crap I had in there."

"I folded my jersey like it was something sacred."

"Spring semester was over."

"No parade. No trophy. Just memories."

"Winning looks good."

"But fighting with everything you have—even when you lose—that stays with you."

Sonny nodded slowly.

"Funny how the best seasons sometimes end in silence."

He looked at me.

"But they still echo."

Act 32: The Jog Begins

"Did you return to New York for the summer?" Sonny asked.

Jervin shook his head.

"I had no plans to return. Christmas left me disappointed. I needed space."

"So, I stayed in Miami."

"Opened my first bank account. Got my first ATM card—and back then, that was a novelty."

"Junior and Rafael's money kept me afloat. I didn't need to work that summer."

Sonny leaned in. "So, what did you do?"

"I kept my routine—jogging every morning. Pull-ups, push-ups, dips."

"Discipline was my anchor."

He paused, eyes narrowing slightly.

"Then one morning… I saw her."

"She was short—about five-four, maybe 115 pounds."

"Long brown hair tied back. Hazel eyes."

"And a stride that said she knew exactly where she was going."

"I was stretching, checking her out discreetly."

"She smiled."

"I smiled back."

"She looked at her watch."

"Then she took off."

"She was too far ahead to catch."

"But I looked at my watch—8:15 a.m."

Okay, I thought to myself, I'll start at 8:00 tomorrow.

Sonny chuckled. "Sounds like stalking."

Jervin laughed. "No—it was more like a scouting report."

They both laughed.

"Sure enough, the next morning—there she was."

 "Stretching. Ready."

"I walked over casually and introduced myself."

"'Hi, I'm Jervin.'"

She paused for a second, then extended her hand.

"'Hi. I'm Becky.'"

"I was a straight shooter. I used to be shy, but time changed me."

"'Listen, Becky—I jog two miles a day, every morning except Sundays. I could use a partner.'"

She raised an eyebrow.

"'Excuse me?'"

"'What I meant was—it makes jogging faster and easier with a partner. I don't have to think too much.'"

"She kept stretching. Paused for a second, then looked at me."

"'What are you thinking about?' she asked curiously."

"'New York. My parents. My best friends. The smell of pizza.'"

Sonny interjected, grinning. "You're a smart man. You didn't mention Anna."

Jervin laughed. "Yeah, I didn't want her thinking I was still carrying a torch for Anna. Anyway, I smiled. She started the conversation."

"'So, you're from New York?'"

"'Born and raised. You?'"

"'I'm from Tampa. Are you in college?'"

"'Yeah. I attend Miami University. I'm on the baseball team.'"

"Her eyes lit up."

"'Really? You just lost the finals. What position do you play?'"

"'I'm the starting shortstop.'"

"She laughed; I was baffled."

"'Oh, so you're the guy that looks like he's dancing when he fields the ball?'"

"I blinked."

"'How do you know that?'"

"'I go to Miami University too. I'm a med student. Studying to be a doctor. My girlfriend calls you the dancer.'"

"When she said girlfriend," Sonny asked, "did you think girlfriend as in female friend, or girlfriend as in partner?"

Jervin shrugged. "To be honest, in 1981, people weren't out like that. It was pretty taboo in certain circles."

"And besides, it never occurred to me. I didn't ask what she meant. I didn't want to assume either."

"I just wanted the moment to breathe."

"So, I grinned."

"'That's funny, because I don't dance. The baseball diamond helps me escape reality. It's like being an actor. You get into character, and when the director says cut, the lights go off.'"

"She nodded."

"'Alright, let's start jogging, Al Pacino. I've got things to do after this jog.'"

"'Don't ever ask me about my business, Kay,' I said, slipping into my best Al Pacino impression."

"She let out a light laugh."

"'Okay,' I said, falling in beside her."

"And just like that, the morning changed."

"The jog wasn't just about movement anymore."

"It was about rhythm. Connection. And the possibility of something new."

"I didn't know if I would see her again."

"But for twenty minutes, I wasn't thinking about New York. Or Anna. Or the finals."

"I was just moving forward."

"Following Mr. Johnson's advice: Move on."

Sonny smiled.

"Funny how a jog can turn into a story."

Act 33: The Next Day

"Did you ever meet with Becky again?" Sonny asked.

Jervin nodded. "Yeah. She took me up on my offer."

"Before the jog, we had a conversation."

"'What part of New York are you from?' she asked."

"'Manhattan. Lower East Side.'"

"'Lower East Side, you say,' she replied in a mock James Cagney voice."

"At least she had a sense of humor."

"'Yeah. Born and raised there. Have you ever been to New York?'"

Becky shook her head. "'No, but I've always wanted to go. I imagine it's loud, fast, and full of stories.'"

I chuckled. I started to notice she had a slight Southern drawl.

"'That's one way of putting it. It has rhythm. You learn to move with it—or get swallowed.'"

I started to paint a picture, gliding my hand in the air like Sofia from *The Golden Girls*.

"'Pizza on every corner. Sirens at night. And people who talk like they're auditioning for a Francis Ford Coppola film.'"

She laughed, and for the first time, I noticed she had dimples.

"'Sounds intense. I love your New York accent. Are you Italian?'"

"'No, but I grew up around Italians. The only thing is—I say three, not tree.'"

She laughed again. She was warming up to me.

"'You sound just like the people I watch on those TV shows based in New York.'"

Sonny grinned. "So, it looks like you were hitting it off."

"Actually, we were," Jervin said.

He continued, "So I told her:

'It's intense. But it's home. Even when I'm not there—it's in me. The way I walk. The way I talk. The way I play ball.'"

She looked at me curiously, like she was trying to figure out what species I was in the animal kingdom.

"'So why did you leave?' Becky asked."

"I paused. Not because I didn't know the answer—but because saying it out loud made it real."

In a softer voice, I answered.

"'Dreams. And the need to prove something to myself, mostly. Miami's got sun. But New York gave me grit.'"

I smiled.

"'Oh yeah—and I also received a scholarship.'"

She laughed at that. Smiled again—this time, a little warmer.

"'I like that. Grit is an underrated quality.'"

I grinned. "Yeah, well… it's all I had for a while."

After stretching, we began to jog. This time, side by side.

She'd occasionally peek in my direction, pretending to be discreet.

And from the corner of my eye, I could see a tiny light flickering in hers—even though I pretended not to notice.

I didn't know what was happening.

But for the first time in a long time—I wasn't jogging alone.

We didn't talk about tomorrow.

But the way she glanced at me said: *Maybe.*

Sonny smiled.

"Sounds like the kind of morning that stays with you."

Act 34: The Counselor's Office

"Did you ever hear from Anna again?" Sonny asked.

Jervin's voice dropped, his eyes drifting somewhere distant.

"Well… I went to the school counselor. She was also a licensed therapist."

"I needed closure. I was conflicted. I needed to know if I had done something wrong—something that made Anna stop reaching out."

"I couldn't shake the feeling that she'd left me behind without explanation."

Sonny nodded. "Sounds like you just needed closure, like you mentioned before."

Jervin nodded. "Yeah. I remember the counselor's office. It wasn't necessarily large—more like an interrogation room."

"Neutral colors. Nothing remarkable."

"There was a plant in the corner that looked like it could use some water."

"I mean, the poor thing looked thirsty."

Sonny chuckled. "Now that's a detail."

Jervin smiled faintly.

"She leaned forward during one part of the session and asked, 'If you were disabled right now, would Anna drop everything and run to your side?'"

"I hesitated. It was a good question. But I pivoted."

"'She picked Harvard,' I said."

"'She did,' the counselor replied. 'But if she really wanted to be with you, she would've come with you to

Miami. You said she was wealthy. Why would it matter—Harvard or Miami University?'"

"I tried to defend Anna."

"'Her father thought it was unsafe to come to Miami. Harvard was better for her future.'"

"The counselor nodded slowly."

"'So, her father made the decisions for her. She said Harvard was better for her future,' the therapist said."

"I waited for the next words with anticipation, my heart pounding."

"'She was thinking about her future. One that did not include you.'"

"I went silent."

"The kind of silence that fills your chest like freezing water."

"It was a verbal flatline. I went speechless."

"I just let the truth settle in—like freezing rain on warm skin."

"I didn't know how to continue the session."

"So I stood up and thanked the therapist."

"As I left, I felt her eyes on me. Not judgmental. Just… empathetic."

"She felt for me. But her job was to be honest."

"And honestly? It hurts."

"But it also cleared the fog."

"It was time to move on."

"Just like Mr. Johnson said. Just like Junior suggested."

Sonny nodded.

"Sometimes the hardest truths are the ones that set you free."

Act 35: Rafael's Confession

"I have to confess something about Rafael," I said.

Sonny leaned in. "I'm all ears."

"Rafael was smooth. Always had a way with words—and women. He went through women like I went through underwear."

"But beneath that charm was a story that didn't end the way it should have."

"One day, I asked him why he never made it to the majors."

"He looked away."

"Not just looked away—he folded into himself, like the memory was heavier than the words."

"Then he said quietly, 'I was drafted by the Montreal Expos.'"

"That surprised me."

"'Got traded to the Phillies. While I was there… I got caught up. Cocaine. Transactions. Usage. I was suspended. I was released. Even after I was exonerated, no team would touch me. I was toxic. Banned.'"

"I didn't know what to say."

"He didn't need pity."

"He needed someone to remember."

"Rafael wasn't just a mentor. He was a man who danced with the dirt and got buried in the system."

"But he stood tall."

"Still, he passed on his wisdom. His life experience. And he believed in me."

"He taught me how to stand tall when the world wants you small."

"He played big brother when I lost my brother Manny."

"I'd seen old photos—him in an Expos uniform. A picture with a young Gary Carter in Single-A ball. They both looked like kids."

"He looked like he belonged."

"And for a moment—he did."

"And that?" I looked at Sonny. "That made him a legend in my book."

"At that moment in time, Rafael's strength helped me prevail."

"If he had been in Miami, he would've told me I was going to be okay."

Sonny nodded slowly.

"Sometimes legends don't need stats. They just need someone to tell the story right."

Act 36: Cheesecake and Confession

"Let's talk about Becky," Sonny said, leaning back in his chair, arms folded like he was settling in for a story.

Jervin nodded, a slow smile tugging at the corner of his mouth. "Okay."

He paused, letting the memory settle before speaking.

"After jogging together for about a month, I finally asked Becky out to dinner. She said, 'Okay.' Just like that. No hesitation. We went to a Cuban spot near South Beach— nothing fancy, but it had soul. I pulled up in my used Oldsmobile Cutlass, financed by Junior and Rafael. The paint was faded, the engine coughed like a smoker in winter, but it was mine."

Sonny chuckled. "Stylish."

"In those days," Jervin continued, "I didn't know jack shit about finance, credit, equity, car insurance, stocks, bonds, money markets, or 401(k)s. I just knew I had a bank account, a car, and a cute girl who said yes."

"During dinner, we started peeling back the layers. Becky told me her dad owned a business in Tampa. She didn't go into detail, but you could tell by the way she dressed—tailored, elegant, like she was used to quality. 'He just wants me to go further in life than he did,' she said. I nodded, thinking, This man set a high ceiling for his daughter."

Jervin's eyes softened.

"She also told me she was Sicilian and Cuban. I said, 'Jesus. Talk about a hot-blooded combination. That's Mount Vesuvius level.' She laughed. I knew right then—don't piss this one off."

Sonny laughed. "Smart man."

"Then she hit me with, 'What's your favorite piece of literature?' I said, 'Death of a Salesman.' She looked surprised. 'Really?' she asked. I told her yes; I could relate to Willie Loman. A man who gave everything to a company, only to be phased out when the owner's son took over. Disillusioned. I'd seen that in my neighborhood—men who were loyal, who gave everything, and got nothing back."

He paused, his voice quieter now.

"And then there's Biff—the college football star. Willie still saw him as that kid, but Biff had changed. I saw that too. Moms bragging about their kids' elementary school awards while those same kids were out on the corner, changing right in front of the world."

Sonny nodded slowly. "Damn."

"Becky just sat there, eating her rice and beans, eyes locked on mine. Then she leaned in and asked, 'What did it teach you?'"

"'I learned to pay attention,' I said. 'And not to get stuck in time. People get stuck. Things change. People change. Seasons change. All of that.'"

She smiled. "'You really thought about this, haven't you? I don't think it's just the story. It's you.'"

Jervin smiled at the memory. "We didn't rush the moment. Just let the conversation settle like sugar in strong coffee. But it was getting a little too deep, so I did what I do best—cracked a joke."

"Of course you did," Sonny said.

"The waiter came by and asked, 'Will you have dessert?' I looked at Becky and said, 'Cheesecake.' She nodded. 'Two slices. Oh, and bring her some more wine—I want to get her drunk.'"

They both laughed. Becky leaned in and asked, "Do you speak Spanish?"

Jervin nodded.

"'Really?' she asked."

"'Sí, mi amor,' I said."

"'Yes,' I added, 'and a little French and Jive.'"

She laughed again. "'You know French? How'd you learn?'"

"'I… took it as a minor in high school,' I said."

That was a total lie. Anna taught me French. But I wasn't about to ruin the moment. Rafael once told me: never mention your ex on a date—especially not with a Latina. That's just asking for an interrogation.

Sonny burst out laughing. "You learned well, my friend."

"Rafael used to say, 'When it comes to women, you have the right to remain silent. Anything you say may be used against you in a future argument.' He called it his Miranda Rights."

"Classic Rafael," Sonny said, wiping a tear from his eye.

"Anyway," Jervin continued, "after dinner, I drove Becky home. The night was warm—the kind that makes you want to linger in the car a little longer. We pulled up to her place. She leaned over and kissed me. 'Tell me something in French,' she whispered."

I smiled, leaned in, and said, "Tu es sexy."

She laughed, kissed me again, and said, "You know, I have my own apartment. You can come in."

I said yes. I mean, she didn't have to twist my arm. But for a second, I just sat there, anchored in the car. My past still had its hooks in me.

She looked back. "You coming?"

"Yes," I said. And meant it.

"I loved being around Becky," Jervin said, his voice low, reflective. "We jogged together every morning. Liked the same music, same movies, same pop culture quirks. She was smart, funny, grounded. But I wasn't in love with her."

He paused, eyes drifting toward the window as if the memory was just outside.

"One day she said, 'I love being around you.' I smiled. Paused. Then said, 'It's fun.' That might've been the wrong answer. But I couldn't lie about my feelings. I couldn't pretend I was madly in love with her. Not after Anna. Not after what silence taught me."

Sonny didn't interrupt. He just listened, the way only old friends know how.

"I started putting up guardrails. Emotional ones. The teen naivety was gone. I was becoming my own man. And my worldview was shifting. I used to watch TV and see these perfect families—dad with a tie, mom with an apron, serving a casserole, kids with clean shoes and clean problems. I'd sit there and think: What a crock of shit."

Jervin chuckled, but there was no humor in it.

"Family and life? They're messy. Complicated. Full of scars, secrets, and moments that don't get solved in thirty minutes. I wish I could resolve my problems in half an hour. But I knew better."

Sonny leaned back, a knowing grin spreading across his face.

"Funny how cheesecake can turn into a confession booth."

Jervin smiled.

"Yeah. Funny like that."

Act 37: Keep It Real

"Okay," Sonny said, leaning forward, elbows on his knees. "Let's talk about the spring of '82."

Jervin exhaled, eyes narrowing as the memory came rushing back.

"The spring of '82 felt like a kid living a fantasy. We were the number one team in the country. Scouts filled the stands. *Sports Illustrated* wrote about me—called me 'the dancing shortstop.' Said I had the potential to be a five-tool player. Junior and Rafael sent clippings, always with a note: 'You're almost there, kid.'"

"I was locked in. Focused on my studies. Chasing a two-year degree—because that's all my scholarship covered. I had to make it here—or go back to New York with nothing but memories and uncertainty."

He paused, then added,

"Becky and I were still dating, but the romance had cooled. Our schedules were brutal. We were two people orbiting different stars."

Jervin leaned back, eyes distant.

"One afternoon, I left practice early and headed to a coffee shop near campus. Croissants, espresso. Study. Plain and simple. My routine. Then I saw Becky with another med student. She was leaning in, and he looked at her like she was the only person in the room. She was dominating the conversation. He was absorbing her every word—like he was in a trance."

"I had two choices: walk in and interrupt this little liaison, or walk away. I walked away. I figured if it meant anything, she'd bring it up. She didn't."

He shook his head.

"Three days passed. I channeled my anger onto the field. I hit like a man possessed. Then I saw her."

"'So, where have you been? I haven't seen you in three days,' I asked, keeping my tone even."

"'Studying for finals,' she said, nonchalantly."

"'Do you have a study partner?' I asked, careful not to tip my hand."

"'What do you mean?' Her tone sharpened."

Rafael's voice echoed in my head: *People who act defensively usually have something to hide.*

"'I passed by the coffee shop the other day. I saw you having a grand ol' time with a guy. Who is he?'"

"'Wait—I can't have male friends?' she snapped."

"'Sure. But this guy looked at you like a puppy waiting to get adopted.'"

"'What are you trying to say, Jervin? Just spit it out. Stop sidestepping.'"

"'Okay. You don't look for me. You don't reach out. I'm searching all over campus and you're nowhere to be found. What do you expect me to think?'"

"'Maybe I'm studying for my finals,' she retorted."

I nodded calmly. Clear.

"'Becky, you know I'm leaving after this championship is over. I'm gone by June. So it doesn't matter at this point. But me and you—it's not going to work.'"

She raised her voice. "Are you seriously breaking up with me?"

She wasn't heartbroken—but her pride was bruised.

"'I'm not saying that. If you want, we could hang. You know where to find me. But right now, I have a championship tournament coming up. That's my focus. Scouts are going to be at our games.'"

I looked at her one last time, then turned and walked away.

"'Jervin!'" she yelled.

I turned around.

"'You really think you're going to be a major leaguer? Pfft. Dude, keep it real!'"

I stared at her. Cold.

That one stung. The "dude" remark? That was a slight. A slap. Her words hit harder than a fastball.

But I didn't flinch.

Because I knew—belief starts inside. And hers was never there.

I turned and walked away. I didn't argue. She never believed in me. But I believed in me. Because I was built on the Lower East Side—where grit wasn't optional.

I just thank God I didn't fall in love with her. That would've been a miserable existence. She showed me her true colors.

Sonny exhaled, shaking his head.

"Sometimes the realest thing you can do is walk away."

Jervin nodded.

"Yeah. And sometimes, that's the only way to win."

Act 38: Omaha

Sonny leaned forward, eyes wide with curiosity. "So, you headed to Omaha, Nebraska—your second consecutive College World Series. Tell us about that."

Jervin smiled, his voice tinged with nostalgia. "We made it to the championship—but first, let me talk about Rico."

He chuckled. "Rico had this way of loosening us up with his comedy routine. It became a ritual. Right before big games, he'd launch into one of his wild stories. This one time he goes:

'Yo, I was looking at two dogs the other day. The male dog went up to the female dog—or we call her, "The Bitch." He started sniffing her ass. So I'm wondering, like imagine if they could talk. He might say something like, "Yo, your shit smells familiar, but I can't picture the face." Then she turns around and says, "Yo, it's me, Chiquita. Remember you fucked me last week?" Then the male dog says, "Yeah, I remember tappin' that ass." And she's like, "Yeah, then you howled when you came, then sat in the corner and licked your balls for five minutes."'"

Jervin laughed. "We were all dying. Couldn't breathe. Rico had that timing, that delivery. He could've been a stand-up comic if baseball didn't work out for him."

Sonny grinned. "Looks like you like comedy."

"Oh yeah," Jervin said. "It keeps me from going insane. There's a difference between being funny and being cruel. Rico knew that line. He danced on it, but he never crossed it."

He paused for a moment, the smile fading into something softer

"The year before... we were simply happy to be there. First time in Omaha. Bright lights, big stage. We were wide-eyed kids with big dreams. But this time? We came to win."

"Coach gave us a day to unwind before the big game," Jervin said, his voice warm with memory. "Said we needed to release pressure. I heard Omaha was famous for arcades—so that's where we went. Walked in and it hit me—Playland on 42nd Street. Junior and I used to spend hours battling pinball machines, chasing high scores. That memory grounded me. Reminded me where I came from."

He paused, then smiled.

"Then came the big day. Wichita State against us. There were mascots, people with face paint, cheerleaders from both sides—the full college circus. Watching a sea of red representing us in the crowd made the stadium electric. I imagined Junior and Rafael were there. But I didn't feel empty. This was the game of my life."

Jervin shook his head, grinning.

"We were up 9–3 in the ninth. Two outs. Wichita hit a soft pop-up. Rico snatched it, and just like that—we were College World Series champions. For a second, no one moved. It felt like time had stood still. Then—an eruption. Like a dam breaking."

He leaned back, eyes misty. "I remember jumping and dogpiling on the mound—just like I saw a year ago, only this time, we were on top. Cameras were flashing. I was holding up my index finger, signaling number one. Then the other guys joined me. That picture of us throwing up the number one made the newspapers, *Sports Illustrated*, and other media outlets."

"Miami was ecstatic. It was their first-ever baseball championship. That day, my exposure grew. The scouts noticed. After the natural high of winning, everything started to move slowly. Like slow motion. It was surreal. I swear I heard 'We Are the Champions' by Queen—but it could've been my imagination. Or maybe it was real."

He paused, voice softer now.

"It was my first championship on any level. The celebration was great, but just like that, my college career was over. I was fulfilled. But I was ready for the next challenge in my life."

Sonny smiled, eyes misty.

"You didn't just win a title. You earned your story."

Act 36: Let It Be

Sonny asked gently, "Out of curiosity… did you see Becky before you left Miami?"

Jervin smiled faintly, the kind of smile that holds both peace and ache.

"Funny story. On my last day on campus, I was packing up two suitcases, a couple of trophies, and a heart that had seen enough. I was loading the car, getting ready to head back to New York. The sun was low, casting long shadows across the parking lot."

"And then I saw her. Becky was alone, walking slowly, like she had nowhere urgent to be. I thought about walking up to her. Saying goodbye. One last conversation. One last moment."

"But then another part of me said… just like the Beatles… let it be."

"I watched her from a distance. Followed her with my eyes until she disappeared around the corner. She never once looked in my direction. Whether it was intentional or not, I'll never know."

"And that was that. I never saw her again."

Sonny tilted his head. "So, your plan was to drive back to New York. Why not fly?"

Jervin grinned. "I drove back because I wanted to take the long way home."

Act 37: Road Trip

"It was two weeks before the Amateur Draft," Jervin began, his voice mellow with memory. "And I figured—why not see parts of America I hadn't seen while I still had the time and the chance?"

Sonny leaned in, listening.

"My first stop was Sanford, Florida. I pulled up to a diner off the highway. It was still early enough to order breakfast. I'd left Miami at the crack of dawn—almost a four-hour drive. I walked in with a smile and headed straight to the counter. The place reminded me of one of those old 1950s diners, but with a few modern touches."

He chuckled.

"Behind the counter stood this older white lady—hairnet, apron, and what I called 'cat-woman glasses.' Thick frames, like magnifying lenses. She looked like she'd been serving coffee since the Eisenhower years."

"'Good morning,' she said, in a Southern drawl, which caught me off guard."

True to form, I hit her with my New York accent.

"'Yes, can I have scrambled eggs, toast, orange juice, coffee—and if you have it, a slice of cantaloupe?'"

She scribbled down my order, then looked up and asked, "You're not from around here, are you?"

"'No, ma'am. I'm from New York.'"

"I swear—the whole diner went silent. Like one of those movie scenes when the record scratches and everyone suddenly gets quiet and stares at you."

Sonny laughed. "Classic."

"There was a quick moment of silence. Then she said, 'I'll bring you your breakfast.'"

"'Okay. Thank you,' I said, trying to keep it light, pretending no one was staring at me. But in my head, I was thinking: What the fuck am I doing?"

"I scanned the diner, and the only open seat was a table with an African American motor cop—aviator shades, badge on his chest, coffee in hand. I figured I'd be safer with him than with the rest of that lovely crowd."

Sonny laughed again. "Smart move."

"So, I sat down. The officer looked at me. Didn't say much—just a nod. And at that moment, I realized something. This wasn't just a road trip. This was a reminder—and a recognition—of where I came from. And how far I still had to go. I was a thousand miles from home."

Sonny nodded, his voice low. "Being alone in the South as a young man in the 1980s is quite an adventure."

Jervin smiled. "Yeah. And that was just the first stop."

Act 38: The Road North

"My next stop was Savannah, Georgia," Jervin said, his voice mellow with memory. "I expected banjo-playing, whiskey-drinking yokels. Stares. That feeling of being an alien in your own country. But Savannah was a cultural haven. The day I arrived, I saw Spanish moss hanging like laces from trees. Cobblestone streets—just like Essex Street. Art galleries tucked between cafés. It had a kind of beauty New York couldn't match—fresh, deliberate, and slow in a way that felt intentional. The South had its own rhythm. Its own care. And in the mornings, the air smelled like mountain dew—not the soda, the actual dew. Sweet. Earthy. Alive."

"I wanted to see what the guys on my block would never see. Back home, the corner crew was still there. Same stoop. Same stories. Gossip was their currency. Their lives measured in reruns. I needed more than that."

He leaned back, eyes scanning the ceiling like it held a map of his journey.

"After Georgia, I kept driving through South Carolina. I stopped at a convenience store and noticed they sold fireworks—just sitting there on the shelf."

"'Are those legal here?' I asked."

"'Yes, they are. As long as you don't cross state lines with them,' the clerk said."

"He was friendly. I bought snacks, and when I paid, I left him a tip."

"'Here's your change, son.'"

"'Keep it. It's okay,' I said."

"Next was North Carolina. I was tired, so I stayed at a hotel in Fayetteville. Early the next morning, the smell of mountain dew opened my lungs. I could breathe naturally. I could get used to this country's mountain air, I thought to myself."

"As I kept driving, I noticed something. The toll booth clerks changed with each state. They were friendly and cheerful in Delaware, Maryland, and Virginia. A little less friendly in Pennsylvania. Even less in New Jersey. The lady in the booth looked hungover, and by the look on her face, she wanted to be left alone. And finally, I reached New York. The token booth lady looked miserable. I was worried she had a gun under her chair."

Jervin laughed softly.

"This was my first real road trip on my own. But for me? It was a challenge. A test. A way to step out of my comfort zone and explore something new. Truthfully, I wanted to see if what people had told me about the South was true. Honestly, there was some truth to the speculation."

"I hadn't been in New York since 1980, so it had been about a year and a half. The skyline rose like an old friend—familiar, flawed, and full of stories. The bridge. The noise. The pulse of the city—it all came rushing back. I rolled down the window of my Cutlass and let the New York air hit my face. It smelled like asphalt, roasted peanuts, and possibility."

"I passed the corner where Junior and I used to hang out as kids. Same guys, just a little older, were there. Same stale-ass stories, just a different decade. I didn't stop to greet any of them. I just kept going. I had trophies in my trunk, a degree in my pocket, and fire in my chest. I was not the naïve kid who left in 1980."

"I had seen Savannah's grace. Sanford's grit. Omaha glory. And plenty of Miami sunshine. I had loved and lost. I had learned to read silence—and swing through doubt. New York hadn't changed much. But I had."

"The draft was days away. George had made me eligible. I wasn't nervous. Because I was ready to swing through whatever came next."

Sonny nodded, eyes full of pride.

"You didn't just take the long way home. You found your way."

Act 39: Draft Day

"So draft day was here," Sonny said, leaning forward. "The day you dreamed about since you were a kid. Tell us about that."

Jervin nodded.

"I called George. Told him, 'Today is the big day.'"

George responded in his usual even-keel tone. "'I know, Jervin. Listen—come to my office. Bring Rafael and Junior. I know they're your support system. I've got a guy who'll be updating me on the draft process.'"

"'A guy who knows a guy?'" I joked, slipping into my best Italian Brooklyn accent.

"'Ha,'" George chuckled.

"'That sounds like a plan,'" I told George. "'And George… my offer still stands,'" I said with purpose.

"'Let's see if you get drafted first. We have to be realistic, kid. Just in case,'" George said, stoic as ever.

We gathered in George's office on Madison Avenue—Junior, Rafael, and me. We talked about everything from baseball to politics to women to food.

"'I could go for a good lasagna,'" George said at one point.

"'Let's order tree,'" I replied, using my wiseguy voice in full effect.

George laughed. I was bringing back the greatest hits of my childhood and teen years. I always joked when I was anxious—when the air got too thick.

We sat for hours, eating knishes and hot dogs from the corner vendor. Drinking cans of Coca-Cola like it was ale on St. Patrick's Day.

Then the phone rang.

The room went silent—the kind of silence you make when your mother tells you to pretend you're not home when annoying neighbors knock on the door. We stared at George like he was holding the balance of the universe in his hand. He scribbled notes on a legal pad, then hung up.

We all started talking at once.

"'Hold on, hold on...'" George shouted, waving his hands. "'I just received breaking info. The Cubs selected Shawn Dunston as the number one overall pick.'"

"'I remember Shawn,'" I said. "'Brooklyn kid. How about the Mets?'"

George scanned the legal pad. "'They picked a kid from Tampa named Dwight Gooden.'"

Upon hearing that, I stood up. I was nervous and decided to take a walk around the block. Get some air. Junior came with me. We grabbed Spanish espresso and sat for about fifteen minutes.

As I sat in the booth, I looked out the window, hoping my dreams weren't going to be a wash.

"'Don't worry, kid,'" Junior said. "'There are like thirty-seven rounds or something like that. So what if it's not the Mets? At least you have a chance at the majors, one way or another.'"

I didn't answer. I couldn't. I just took a deep breath. Deep. Slow. Trying to keep my anxiety from boiling over.

After a pause, I said, "'Okay. Let's go.'"

As we walked back to George's office, a car passed by playing "Another One Bites the Dust" by Queen, and I had to laugh to myself. Junior walked in silence beside me. Becky's voice echoed in my head: *Keep it real, dude.*

Now I was getting annoyed. My face was stoic, with a tinge of anger.

When we walked into George's office, George and Rafael were sitting apart on a sofa. They looked like two men in a maternity waiting room, hoping for good news.

"'So… anything?'" I asked.

George looked at his legal pad. "'The Mets made their number two pick,'" he said.

"'Yeah? Who'd they take?'" I asked, tension creeping into my voice.

"'Some scrub,'" George said. "'His name is…'" He paused. "'Jervin Class.'"

Junior screamed. Rafael and George burst out laughing. They were fucking with me—and honestly, it was working.

But the news stunned me. I had to sit down and gather myself. My eyes welled up. Finally, someone recognized me.

But crying? Out of the question.

Because remember—there's no crying in baseball.

Act 40: The Call

Sonny leaned back, a slow smile spreading across his face. "You didn't get drafted," he said. "You arrived."

Then he leaned in, voice soft, almost reverent. "So, what was your next move? Your dream of getting drafted was now a reality. What did you do next?"

Jervin exhaled, his eyes narrowing with memory.

"You know, for the first time in my life, I wasn't chasing the dream. I was the dream."

He paused, letting the words settle.

"I sat for a minute, letting it all sink in. All those years of sweat. George helping me perfect my swing. Rafael teaching me how to dance with the dirt. Junior toughening me up. It all paid off. It led to that day."

He leaned forward, elbows on his knees.

"Then reality hit. Next came the minor leagues. Long bus rides. Cheap meals. Dingy motels. It stripped the glamour right out of the moment. But I wasn't afraid. It was just the next challenge. And I was ready to swing through whatever came next."

He looked down at his hands, then back up.

"Back on the block, the same guys were still there. Same stoop. Same stale stories. Only now, they'd be talking about me. Pretending they knew me personally."

He smiled, but it didn't reach his eyes.

"My next move was obvious. I called my parents. Figured they'd be excited. I mean, I was finally living the dream. Everything I worked for had finally come to fruition."

He shook his head.

"The phone rang a couple of times. Then my father picked up. He had just beaten cancer and insisted on going back to work. Wore himself out. He still looked tired. But when he answered, his voice wasn't warm. Not even curious. Just suspicious."

"'What happened?' he asked. No 'How you doing?' No 'Congratulations.' He sounded like I was calling from a precinct needing bail money."

Jervin's jaw tightened.

"He was always like that. Every call felt like an interrogation. And the thing is, I never asked him for a dime. Two years in Miami, and Rafael and Junior looked out for me. Without them, I wouldn't have made it."

He took a breath.

"The older he got, the more miserable he became. I vowed to break the cycle. Manny was the first hope, but he got stopped in his tracks. Now I was the next one. I didn't want to be another man who settled for less. I wanted to be a cog in the machine—not the one building it with bare hands and broken dreams."

He looked away, voice low.

"'The Mets drafted me as their number two pick,' I told him, expecting at least a flicker of pride."

"'Okay. Good for you. What do you want from me?' he answered."

I hung up the phone.

Jervin's voice caught for a moment, but he pushed through.

"I tried not to show my hurt around the guys. But when the one person you want approval from just… disappoints you—it hits different. He never praised me. He only gave me grief. And yet, I respected him."

He leaned back, eyes distant.

"Jerry Class Jr. came to New York from Sicily in the early fifties. Didn't speak a word of English. Taught himself to read and write. Never finished high school, but he made it work."

"My mother, Rosa Irrizary, came to New York as a child. Didn't speak English either. She was held back one grade. Teachers treated her like she was slow. But she wasn't. She just didn't understand the language. She fought. She learned. Graduated alongside Junior's mother. Then she enrolled in college and earned a bachelor's degree. That was rare for a Puerto Rican woman in the 1960s. She became a teacher. And the irony? She taught Spanish-speaking kids how to speak English."

He smiled, bittersweet.

"I looked up to her. But I couldn't stay around anymore. My father was becoming a detriment to my progress. That phone call changed me. I realized I had to create distance. His silence was louder than any scream. I loved him. But I had to move on. Because dreams don't wait for permission."

He looked at Sonny, voice steady now.

"When I hung up, the guys in the room knew that call was painful. Rafael clapped my shoulder. Junior nodded. They didn't say much. They didn't have to."

"The minor leagues were waiting. And more than ever, I wasn't afraid. I had already faced the hardest pitch life could throw."

Sonny nodded slowly, his voice barely above a whisper.

"Sometimes the hardest part of growing up is realizing who won't grow with you."

Act 41: The Signing

"Okay, let's talk about signing with the Mets," Sonny said, his voice tinged with admiration.

Jervin leaned back, a slow grin forming. "True to my word, I had George negotiate my signing bonus. On a June afternoon, we were invited to Shea Stadium to finalize the deal. While George was inside crunching numbers with the Mets brass, a staff member gave me a tour of the stadium."

He chuckled. "She was young, cheerful—fresh out of college. She was rattling off facts like I was a kid from Iowa seeing a big-league park for the first time. I let her go on for a while. She pointed to the outfield, told me about the history, the legends, the roars of the crowd. The 1969 Mets. Cleon Jones making the final catch. Jerry Koosman on the mound."

Jervin's voice softened. "As we made our way down to the field, we passed the dugouts. I imagined sitting there, cleaning my cleats, putting pine tar on my bat, slamming my helmet on the ground in frustration. It didn't feel distant anymore. It felt possible."

He smiled. "I stood behind home plate, just taking it all in. The field looked massive from ground level. The young woman kept talking, but I interrupted her.

'I grew up in New York,' I said. 'I used to come here as a kid.'

She paused. Blinked. Then smiled back—her tone a little softer, less rehearsed."

After the tour, George and I were invited to lunch with the Mets brass. Before we sat down, George pulled me aside.

"'Jervin,' he said, 'I got you a $100K signing bonus. We're scheduled to sign the contract after lunch.'"

I nodded. "'Good job, George. And you get 15%, correct? That's 15K.'"

George grinned. "'You were always good at math, kid.'"

We toasted my first contract with a glass of champagne. One executive looked at me and asked, "'Are you old enough to drink?'"

It got quiet. Then they all started laughing. All I could say was—it was sweet.

Lunch with the brass. A six-figure bonus. A seat at the table. A month earlier, I was eating Cup of Soup. Today? Filet mignon.

I wasn't just a kid from the Lower East Side anymore. I was a member of the New York Mets.

Sonny smiled, eyes gleaming. "From the stoop to Shea. That's a hell of a signature."

Act 42: The Safe

Later that day, I walked into Jerry's Sporting Goods. Rumor had it Rafael and Junior had purchased 50% of the store. I wanted to see it for myself. Jerry, I was told, was semi-retired.

When I entered the store, the place looked different—modern. It wasn't that dusty 1950s relic I used to work in with Junior. Now it had a slick 1980s vibe. Neon signs. Clean shelves. New cash registers. Not one, but three. Junior and Rafael had upgraded everything.

I looked around, curious. "Has business been that good that you guys can afford this?" I asked.

Junior shrugged. "Yeah, business is good."

I wasn't convinced. Something didn't sit right. Finally, my suspicion got the best of me.

"Come on. This is me. Don't lie to me."

A short silence followed. Rafael walked to the entrance, locked the door, and flipped the sign to CLOSED. We headed to the back of the store, past the racks and the stockroom. A safe was hidden behind workout equipment. Had it always been there? Or was it placed there for a certain purpose?

Rafael opened the safe. "Look inside," he said.

I did. And to my surprise—shock, really—there was at least a quarter million dollars in cash, maybe more. My mind raced. I'd seen stacks of bills on TV, in movies, in stories. But never in real life.

I turned to them, speechless. Finally, I blurted out, "Whatever you're doing… I'll buy 50% of the business. You need to clean that money. I'm your ticket out. Just please stop what you're doing. I love you all. You're the only family I have…"

I stopped. They looked at each other. Then Rafael smiled and placed a hand on my shoulder.

"Jervin, you're acting like your father. Junior hit the lottery. Two-point-five million dollars. If you want in, we can help you buy out Jerry."

"Holy shit! What the fuck! Junior, you're a millionaire!" I yelled.

Junior smiled. "Rafael and I are planning to start something called branding. We're going to create our own designs—batting gloves, T-shirts, jerseys, hats, sports gear. We talked to George. He said to patent everything. We've got people lined up. It's a great idea. You could wear the gear—sweatbands and gloves. With your name on the store, sales could explode."

These guys actually had a business plan. I majored in business at Miami University, so it was time to put my degree to work.

"I'll talk to George. We'll do the paperwork. But we have to buy Jerry out. If anyone can get the deal done—it's George."

"If not, we'll give him an offer he can't refuse," said Junior.

"What you going to do? Cut his cat's head off and leave it at the foot of his bed?"

We all laughed.

"Okay, mi Hermano," Junior said.

"One thing, Junior. Who were those guys I saw you with the day you dropped me off, the last time I was here?" I asked.

"Oh, those guys. Those are my crazy cholo cousins from East L.A. They're from the Mexican side of the family.

They look scary, but they're good guys," Junior said, trying to reassure me.

I felt relieved. I'd thought Junior was into something nefarious. But with this conversation, just like that, I was already a businessperson at twenty. It was also a solid contingency plan in case baseball didn't work out.

This was my family, and I trusted them and their ideas. They were creative guys. I gave them their props. Not only that, but they had game and hustle.

Sonny nodded. "From shortstop to storefront, in one day. That's how you build a legacy."

Act 43: From Shea to Kingsport

"What was next on your agenda?" Sonny asked.

"After signing the bonus," Jervin began, "Junior offered me a place to stay. I wasn't going back to my parents' apartment—not with my father still brooding in the housing projects. He had no plans of moving, and the light in his eyes seemed to have dimmed."

He smiled faintly. "Junior's apartment was clean, spacious, bright. Two bedrooms, two bathrooms. I looked around and joked, 'Oh shit, you're keeping up with the Estefans.'"

"'Who the fuck are the Estefans?' Junior asked.

"'They're big in Miami. They haven't hit New York yet,' I said, matter-of-factly."

Junior brushed off my remark and got down to business. "'Okay, Jervin. Let me ask you a question. After George gets his cut, what do you have left?'"

"'About 85K. I can get a loan against that. Why?'"

Junior grinned. "'Forget that. You need to learn about financing a car. Upgrade your ride. Get rid of that piece of shit you're driving. That thing looks like a grandpa's car. You're never going to get any pussy in that piece of shit—unless you've got some weird geriatric fetish.'"

I laughed. "'Let's go out and get you a nice 1982 Dodge Mirada. You're in a real league now. You have to represent. You have to look the part.'"

A couple of days later, the Mets invited me and the top five picks to Shea. I brought Rafael and Junior along for the ride. George had cases to deal with. They'd earned the right to be part of the moment.

I was introduced to the 1982 Mets roster—Hubie Brooks, Mookie Wilson, Mike Scott, Rusty Staub. The other veterans weren't exactly welcoming. George Foster was salty—lukewarm would be generous. Dave Kingman seemed disinterested. But Rusty Staub was warm. I remembered watching him back in '73 when the Mets made a pennant run and lost to Oakland in seven games. It was a thrill to finally meet him.

The Mets broadcaster interviewed us. We gave the usual generic answers, kept everything in the realm of baseball, smiled and nodded, hoping it would be short. It was strange. I'd never been interviewed before.

After the pre-game jargon, I sat next to Dwight Gooden, the top pick before me. I introduced myself. He looked like he was fourteen with a grown man's body. Quiet. Focused. Rafael, Junior, and I stayed for five innings, then left.

"'Man, they suck,' Rafael said.

"'Maybe they'll turn it around,' I replied, trying to sound optimistic."

Rafael gave me that *I doubt it* look.

A week later, George called me at Junior's apartment.

"'Yeah, George. What's happening?' I asked.

"'Jervin, you've been assigned to Kingsport,' he said.

"'Kingsport. That's great, George. Only one question—where the fuck is Kingsport?'"

George laughed. "'It's in Tennessee.'"

I paused. "'Maybe I'll see the ghost of Elvis.'"

"'Well, that's Memphis. But Elvis's ghost travels,' George said, still laughing."

Later, Junior pulled out his *World Almanac*—our Wikipedia back in 1982. He wanted to give me a background on where I was headed.

"'It's a developing town and community. Doesn't sound bad,'" Junior said.

The day came. Time to leave for my next journey. I looked around Junior's place one last time. He walked me to my car. We shook hands, hugged. He held my suitcase and told me to open the trunk. After placing it inside, he tapped the car. As I started the engine, he passed by my window.

"'Good luck, kid.'"

I took a deep breath. And as I drove away, I never looked in the rearview mirror.

And just like that, I was on my way to Kingsport, Tennessee.

Sonny smiled. "From Shea to Kingsport. That's how dreams start to stretch."

Act 44: Kingsport Heat

"So, tell us about Kingsport?" Sonny asked.

"I drove to Kingsport in my new Dodge Mirada. The car gleamed like a promise. I was twenty, drafted, and ready to prove myself. When I arrived, I met my new teammates—kids, really. A 17-year-old Dwight Gooden, already throwing like a man possessed. A 19-year-old Randy Myers—wild and electric. The game was faster than college. The reality was, we were just prospects. No guarantees unless you perform.

But my college experience paid off. I started off hot. Most of these pitchers had just come out of high school. My glove at shortstop was sharp. My bat was alive. The brass was beginning to notice. They were feeling good about drafting me as high as they did. I was paying dividends.

Baseball was good. But socially, Kingsport was a different world. The town's population was about the size of the housing projects on the Lower East Side. I wasn't used to small towns. I wasn't used to strangers saying, 'Good morning.' In New York, 'Good morning' from a stranger usually meant, 'You got change?' or 'You got a cigarette?'

Kingsport was a tight community. Insular. A handful of fans crossed the line—and there were racist ones. But that could happen in New York too. Minorities always had to deal with that bullshit. It's how you managed it that mattered.

One day, I was in the on-deck circle. I took off my helmet, my thick black hair slicked back, looking like a Puerto Rican Pat Riley. A guy shouted, 'Oh shit, these Mutts got Ricky Ricardo!' Another chimed in, 'Lucy, you got some spaining to do!'

I stood stunned for a moment. Naively, I thought America was past this. But I should have known better. Brandon reminded me in high school that this still existed.

Later in the game, the heckler started again. The first time, I didn't turn around. The second time, I did. He was a heavyset white guy, mid-thirties, looked like he hadn't missed a meal since the Nixon years. He started with 'Lucy… Lucy…' in an exaggerated Cuban accent.

So I turned around and pointed at him. In my best Ricky Ricardo impression, I said, 'Is that so ridiculous!'

A bunch of fans laughed. I smirked and turned back around. He started cursing, but I ignored him. He was getting under the skin of other fans. One fan yelled, 'Hey, sit your fat ass down and shut the fuck up!' They went back and forth for a while until security came and tried to calm the situation.

After the game, the manager pulled me aside.

"'Ignore them,' he said. 'You're going to hear that bullshit as long as you play.'

"'I'm not my grandfather,' I snapped. 'I'll fuck that fat fuck up.'"

The manager nodded, then softened. He put a hand on my shoulder.

"'I get it, kid. But this is about your career. You don't want to blow it. One day, who knows, you might get a platform and you can blow off steam. But right now, it's not the time.'

"He paused. 'Remember, an eye for an eye leaves the world blind.'

"'Who said that?' I asked.

"'Martin Luther King, Gandhi, Nurse Ratched—who gives a fuck. The point is, you can't control who loves you or who hates you. I know you may not understand that now, but you will. You can't control people's feelings—only your own. I hope you get my point.'"

He was actually dropping pearls of wisdom. It was up to me to absorb them.

The experience brought me back to something that happened when I was a kid with Manny. Once, we put change in the bus fare slot. For some reason, the driver singled us out and said we didn't pay.

"'We paid the fare,' we told him."

He refused to move the bus.

As a ten-year-old, I couldn't understand why this man was treating us like that. As if we were criminals. It got to the point where white ladies on the bus reached into their purses and offered us change to pay the fare.

"'No, we paid our fare,' I told them, refusing their money."

The driver still wouldn't budge. Finally, Manny said, "'We're not going to win this battle. Let's go.'"

I looked at the ladies. They felt bad. They knew what was happening. It wasn't about the fare. It was about who we were.

My ten-year-old self turned to the driver. "'Fuck you, asshole,'" I said, flipping him the bird.

That moment with the fan reminded me—the world hasn't changed. But I have to find a way to manage it.

Despite it all, I was batting .350. The brass noticed. They promoted me to Lynchburg for the 1983 season. Kingsport would be behind me. A new team. A new town.

The experience in Kingsport just made my skin thicker.

Sonny nodded. "You didn't just play through the rain and heat in Kingsport. You learned to stay cool."

Act 45: Lynchburg Bound

"Let's talk about Lynchburg," Sonny said.

"It was January of 1983," Jervin began. "I was sitting in Junior's condominium—legs stretched out, flipping through a real estate flyer. I was thinking about buying a condo myself. I had the money—barely—but I wanted to be sure. Rafael and Junior offered to help. George said he'd manage the closing if I decided to go down that path.

One thing about being a ballplayer—you can call an abundance of places home. Some are temporary. Others permanent. Most fall somewhere in between. Some of us are just rolling stones."

Junior was my *World Almanac*. My encyclopedia. He described Lynchburg like a travel agent with a sense of humor.

"'It's located in the foothills of the Blue Ridge Mountains along the James River,'" he read aloud.

"'Sounds like a brochure for a summer camp,' I joked. 'Sounds like a PBS pledge drive. I'm about to donate money to you.'"

Junior half-laughed. The *World Almanac* was our Google back then. Our Wikipedia. Our lifeline to places we'd never seen.

As a joke, I called George back after he told me I was promoted to Lynchburg.

"'Where the fuck is Lynchburg?' I asked.

George laughed. 'You'll find out soon enough.'"

We liked joking. It kept our relationship professional—but friendly. But deep down, I knew Lynchburg wasn't just a town. It was a test.

Lynchburg had future major leaguers—Lenny Dykstra and Dwight Gooden. I called Dykstra my Little Psycho. I loved the way he played. He was hard as, well, Nails. I was promoted along with Gooden. I hoped he wasn't thinking I was stalking him. Calvin Schiraldi was also on the team—but more on him later.

The game went up a notch. With each level, it picked up speed. Players were more polished. Curveballs were sharper. The margin of error thinner. Every guy on every team had once been the best player in their high school, their county, their city, their state. All of us were here because someone believed we could someday be major leaguers.

Not all of us were going to make it.

For me, this was a proving ground. Pass this test, and Triple-A was next.

Sonny nodded. "Lynchburg wasn't the big leagues, but it was the proving ground."

Act 46: BIC INK

"Let's talk about BIC INK," Sonny said.

"Around early January of 1983, George finalized the deal to buy Jerry's 50% stake," Jervin began. "We gave Jerry a decent offer—more than it was worth. But we had bigger plans, so the extra cash was worth the investment. We felt 'Sporting Goods' was too narrow. Too bland. Too old school. The world was changing. Culture was shifting. Workout culture was booming—thanks to Jane Fonda tapes, neon sweatbands, and Olivia Newton-John's 'Physical.' A light bulb went off. We wanted in."

He smiled at the memory.

"One cold evening, Junior, Rafael, and I sat in Junior's condo brainstorming ideas. We sat for a couple of hours until Junior finally said, 'Fuck it, I'm hungry. Let's order some Domino's.' We were tossing ideas around like batting practice when the bell rang. Our pizza was here. We ordered six pies."

"'Watch it, Rafael will eat all our food,' I joked."

When Rafael opened his box, I looked at it and said, "'Whoa, what the fuck! Pineapple and bacon? What the fuck is wrong with you?'"

"'What? I like pineapple on my pizza,' Rafael said."

Junior shook his head. "'Nobody likes pineapple on their pizza. That shit is not normal.'"

"'We need to do an intervention,' I said."

"'Fuck you guys,' Rafael shot back."

We all started laughing.

"'How was the food in the minors?' Rafael asked."

"'As bad as when you were in the minors. I stopped eating pork,' I said."

"'Seriously? Why?'"

"'I don't know. For some reason, it started to disgust me.'"

"'Did you hit any Shoney's down south?' Rafael asked."

"'Yes. Their pancakes are the size of an LP—like twelve inches. And you get four,' I told him."

"'Alright, let's get back to business,' Junior said, always focused on the prize. 'I was thinking this: branding—sweatshirts, sneakers, sweatbands, wristbands, accessories, socks. You know, sports gear and wear.'"

We paused. That was a brilliant idea.

"'Okay, I have an idea for the name,' I said. 'How about BIC INK?'"

"'Why that name?' Junior asked."

"'It's an acronym. B is for Blanco—Rafael's last name. I is for your hideous name, Ignacio. And C for Class.'"

"'My name's not hideous,' Junior joked."

"'Well, it's not IBM,' Rafael said. 'But it's ours. We can patent it.'"

We imagined BIC INK on sweatbands in dugouts, on jackets in music videos, on people with cash giving it credibility. We weren't just trying to create a brand. We were trying to create a movement.

We felt confident in our ability. I felt especially confident in Rafael and Junior. Those guys were creative.

After the meeting, the next day I flew out to Puerto Rico and played a couple of weeks in the winter league. It wasn't really on my agenda, but I got a call to play shortstop for one of the teams. It was nice to be back in warm weather—even if it was only for two weeks.

Act 47: Spring Training Call

"After two weeks in Puerto Rico, I was back in New York, braving the brutal cold," Jervin said. "I was on my third cup of coffee, I think. I was alone—Junior had gone to Boston to visit family. I admired his condo in Manhattan. I wanted one myself someday. I walked toward the window just as a light snowfall began to blanket the city. The snow made the skyline feel picturesque."

He paused, letting the memory settle.

"Later on, I was watching television, but mostly just staring into space. I was a little worn from my flight. Then the phone rang. I picked it up—George was on the other end."

"'Jervin, I received a call from the Mets.'"

My first thought? I was either traded or released.

"'Yes, and?' I said."

"'Let me finish,' George replied. 'The Mets are inviting you to spring training as a non-roster invitee.'"

Holy shit, I thought.

"'Really?'" It was all I could manage.

"'Now, Jervin, you have zero chance of making the team out of spring training—but you can display your talent. They know who you are. Let them know you want it bad,' George said."

"'I'm aware of that. I've watched baseball long enough,' I told him. 'But I'm going to show them I want to be their shortstop of the future.'"

With every call, it felt like the next best thing in my life was unfolding. The dream of being a big leaguer wasn't a fantasy anymore. Florida. Spring training. Life was sweet.

I was already thinking about my business venture—how I could expose some of our merchandise in Florida. I remember calling Junior in Boston, then Rafael. They were excited for me, but they also saw a major opportunity to capitalize on the situation.

I figured, in two weeks, I'd be around big leaguers. How thrilling was that?

Sonny smiled. "That had to be the thrill of your life."

Jervin just nodded.

Act 48: Meeting Seaver

"Tell us when you met the legend," Sonny said.

"Junior, Rafael, and I took a road trip together," Jervin began. "People used to call us the Three Amigos, and the name stuck. We laughed about it—but there was truth to it. Three guys bound by loyalty, hustle, and a shared dream. Rafael and Junior had more capital than me at that point. They had a small fortune in the vault. We discussed hiring some employees to work in the business. It was the first step in our projects."

"We took turns driving, and before we knew it, we were in Fort Lauderdale, Florida. It was March of 1983. For Rafael and Junior, it would be two weeks of sun, stories, and the kind of freedom we used to imagine. For me, I'd be in the back fields until it was time for Lynchburg."

"The first day of camp, I was suited up, excited about being around the big leaguers. I was tying my cleat, and when I looked up, Tom Seaver was passing. He gave us all a nod and kept walking. I froze for a second. I'm sure Seaver had seen hundreds of kids like me—wide-eyed and hoping. He probably thought I was a clubhouse worker when I first entered the park, until I suited up."

"This guy was a living icon. The anchor of the Miracle Mets. Three-time Cy Young Award winner. The face of the franchise. The soul of Shea Stadium. For a second, I was that kid in the upper deck again, keeping score in my scorebook. I was pissed off in 1977 when the Mets traded him to Cincinnati. I never went back to Shea. And ironically, my next trip to Shea could be as a player."

"George Foster greeted us. Former MVP with the Cincinnati Reds. He looked more like a linebacker than a ballplayer. He was a little warmer this time."

"But Seaver? He was the man. When he walked, he didn't walk—he commanded space. Reporters and players alike made room for him."

"Then there was Darryl Strawberry. He was the second biggest thing in spring training. The overall pick for the Mets in 1980. A big deal. The number one prospect. Cameras followed him everywhere. I was like 16th on the depth chart."

"Rusty Staub was there too. I still remembered him as that right fielder in the 1973 World Series, giving a gallant effort with an injured right shoulder."

"I was getting prepared to face real pitching in a couple of days. I looked straight out toward centerfield and started thinking about my father. We didn't agree on much, but one thing we had in common was baseball. I was starting to miss him because he wasn't there for my big moment. I was hoping that somehow, he'd turn on the TV, see me playing in spring training, and give me a call."

"At the end of the day, my aspiration was to try and be relevant—and work from there. Rafael once told me, 'You don't chase legends. You become one.'"

Sonny nodded. "You didn't need to meet the legend. You stood in his orbit. And that's enough to change a man."

Act 49: The Show

"What was your next adventure?" Sonny asked.

Jervin leaned back, eyes flickering with memory. "Well," he began, "I was given a few at-bats in spring training. I only played with and against some major leaguers.

The few pitchers I faced were Triple-A prospects. I managed two hits, and then it was extended spring training—which means you're cut and waiting for your trip to Lynchburg."

He paused, letting the words settle.

"In April, I arrived at Lynchburg. The team was on fire, and I was hitting around .400. I was raking, hitting for more power. It was like a light turned on in my head. Every swing felt like survival. I didn't take anything for granted. I liked being around big leaguers, and I wanted to get there as fast as possible. The brass took notice and promoted me to Triple-A Tidewater."

A smile crept across his face.

"That night, I called Junior. 'Junior, I can't believe it, but I've just been promoted to Tidewater,' I told him."

He didn't hesitate. "'You're almost there, kid,'" he said.

"When I arrived at Tidewater, the roster was stacked with future major leaguers—Wally Backman, Darryl Strawberry, Ron Darling, and Walt Terrell. These were the big boys. And within a month, Strawberry was promoted to the majors."

"Then in June, the Mets traded for Keith Hernandez. That surprised me. I remembered watching the World Series with Junior and Rafael—Hernandez singling in the sixth inning with the bases loaded, driving in key runs in Game 7."

"'Now that's what you call a clutch hitter,'" Rafael said.

"I was hitting about the same in Tidewater as I was at Lynchburg. Then the Mets' shortstop went down with an injury. I figured one of the other shortstops would get the call, and I'd get a September look."

"A day later, the manager called me into his office. For a moment, I thought the Mets had traded me to get an experienced shortstop. That happens all the time."

"'Congratulations, kid,' the manager said. 'You made the Show.'"

I blinked. "'I'm going to the majors?'"

"'Yes. Pack your bags. You're leaving tonight. A car is going to pick you up, and you're heading to Chicago.'"

I stood there, stunned. "'Thank you. I don't know what to say.'"

The manager was Davey Johnson.

As I packed, I thought of Becky. I yelled into the air, "Fuck you, bitch. It's real!" One of the players looked at me sideways. I just shrugged. "It's a personal thing."

Sonny smiled. "You must have been in heaven."

Jervin nodded slowly. "I was floating. I was heading to Wrigley Field."

Act 50: Wrigley

Sonny leaned forward, his voice carrying the weight of curiosity.

"So tell us about your first adventure in Wrigley?"

Jervin's eyes lit up, and his words came with the rhythm of memory.

"I landed in Chicago and was driven straight to the park. The Sears Tower loomed above me, and to me, it was the equivalent of seeing the World Trade Center for the first time. When I arrived at Wrigley and stepped onto the field, I saw the ivy crawling across the outfield walls. It was surreal. I remember being a kid, rushing home from school to catch the Cubs versus Mets on TV. Back then, the Cubs were the only team without lights, which I always thought was strange.

"The fans—those fans are something else. They support their team through wins, losses, rain, or snow. That day, I was batting eighth in the lineup. My first pitch was from Ferguson Jenkins, a future Hall of Famer. I was nervous. I had never played in front of a crowd that big. He struck me out.

"But the second at-bat, I caught one of his fastballs. I launched it into left-center, and it landed in the stands. The Cubs fans have this tradition of throwing the opposing player's home run ball back onto the field. Lucky for me, because I wanted that ball. That became my first official piece of memorabilia."

Jervin paused, his voice softening as he relived the moment.

"When I reached the dugout, I was buzzing with excitement. But no one congratulated me. Not even eye contact. I sat at the end of the bench, confused. Then Darryl Strawberry walked over, sat beside me, and said, 'You know we're just fucking with you.' Suddenly, Hernandez, Foster, Staub, Mookie—even Seaver came over, patting me on the back. 'Good job, kid.' I was over the moon. For the first time, I didn't feel like a prospect. I felt like a peer."

He leaned back, smiling at the memory.

"That night, I called Junior and Rafael. I was more excited than a Little Leaguer. They told me they'd been watching from the store, and when the ball cleared the fence, they erupted. A customer asked what was going on, and Rafael said, 'He owns half this store.' That endorsement boosted sales."

Sonny nodded, his voice warm with admiration.

"That must have been the thrill of your life."

Jervin's gaze grew distant, his tone almost reverent.

"Words can only describe half of what I felt. The other half lives in emotion."

Act 51: Shea

"Tell us about your first experience at Shea," Sonny said, leaning forward, eyes gleaming.

Jervin exhaled slowly, as if summoning the memory from deep within.

"Yes," he said. "Like I told you before, I hadn't been to a Mets game since 1977—since they traded Seaver. That trade broke something in me. I stopped going. I stopped believing."

Harry Albino

He paused, then smiled faintly.

"And here I was, six years later, playing my first game at Shea—with Seaver on the mound."

He shook his head, still in awe.

"I remember that first at-bat like it's etched in my soul. I stepped into the box and just stood there for a moment, letting it all wash over me. The crowd. The lights. The smell of peanuts and possibility. I could feel the pulse of the city in my chest."

He looked off, as if seeing it all again.

"I scanned the stands, wondering if someone from the block was watching. Wondering if my father was watching, sitting on the same couch, criticizing my stance, my swing—the way we used to joke and tear apart players on TV."

A beat passed.

"Then the umpire barked, 'Batter up!' and I snapped out of it. Came back to earth. I still had a game to play."

He smiled again, this time with quiet pride.

"But do you know what? That time, the results didn't matter. I was playing at Shea. That was more than I could ever dream of."

Act 52: Star Struck

"So, you're in the Major Leagues," Sonny said. "What was going through your mind?"

Jervin leaned back, a grin tugging at the corners of his mouth.

"One thing about the big leagues—you get to stay at luxurious hotels. The food is good. You fly first class. And you travel to places you only dreamed about as a kid."

He chuckled softly.

"Every team we faced was like a roll call of legends. When we played the Phillies, they had Steve Carlton, Pete Rose, Joe Morgan, Tony Perez, and Mike Schmidt. And one of my childhood favorites—Tug McGraw. Part of the '69 Miracle Mets. As a kid in Little League, I tried doing the Pete Rose belly flop. Almost broke a rib."

He shook his head, laughing at the memory.

"In Houston, there was Nolan Ryan. Another Miracle Met. His fastball felt like it broke the sound barrier. I swear, I could hear it pop into Jerry Grote's mitt like a gunshot."

"In Cincinnati, Johnny Bench was retiring. We used to joke about him as kids. Whenever someone didn't get picked in a pickup game, they'd ask, 'Where am I playing?' And we'd say, 'Johnny Bench.'"

He paused, eyes twinkling.

"Davey Concepcion—man, the way he bounced the ball off that turf like magic. I tried that once in Little League. The fields were so bad, the ball died halfway. Pissed off my coach. Never tried it again."

"St. Louis had Jim Kaat, Bruce Sutter, and of course, the Wizard of Oz—Ozzie Smith. I studied him. The way he got to the ball, his footwork, the quick release. Of course, I could never do backflips."

He laughed again.

"In L.A., there was Fernando Valenzuela. In San Diego, a young Tony Gwynn—one of the best hitters I ever saw. He was a rookie in '83 too. In Montreal, that team was stacked: Gary Carter, Andre Dawson, Tim Raines. Future Hall of Famers. Pittsburgh had Dave Parker. That man played like a freight train."

Jervin's voice softened.

"After I did my tour around the league with the legends, I realized something. I had to prove I was a peer—not just an admirer. In my rookie season, I batted .280, hit twelve home runs, and stole fifteen bases. My defense was solid, stellar at times. I was on my way."

He looked down for a moment.

"I always wondered if anybody from the old neighborhood was watching. If they saw me on TV. If they remembered the kid with the glove too big for his hand. But no matter what, I remembered what Rafael once told me: 'Respect the game, and it will respect your back.'"

Sonny smiled. "You didn't meet the legends. You became part of their story."

Act 53: Then I Saw Him

"You told me this part is a little heartfelt. Let's hear it," Sonny said.

Jervin nodded, his voice low. "That fall, I sat in my living room, replaying the moment in my head. I finally purchased the condo of my dreams and had my own place, finally. It was the last Mets home game of the season. I hit a home run. Nothing monumental—the team was going nowhere—but I was trying to make a mark. Trying to prove I belonged."

He paused, eyes distant.

"As I rounded second base, I looked up into the half-empty stands. It was a breezy afternoon, the kind that made flags ripple and shadows stretch across the field. And then I saw him.

Jervin's voice caught for a second.

"My father. Sitting alone. Windbreaker zipped to the neck. Mets cap pulled low. Our eyes locked—just for a second. I had no idea what he was thinking. My father wasn't one for feelings or words. He expressed himself in subtleties. I can't even remember the last time he hugged me."

He looked down at his hands.

"I wondered—was this his way of extending an olive branch? Or was he really proud of me? After the high fives in the dugout, I sat in the corner, quiet. For a moment, I felt like I was ten again."

He exhaled slowly.

"After the game, I rushed to get dressed and ran to the parking lot, hoping to find him. But he was gone. Just like that. I started wondering—had the cancer come back?

Did he want to tell me something? Or did he just want to see me play, one last time?"

Jervin shook his head.

"I didn't know what to think. Should I call him? Visit him? I didn't know. But when the season ended, I knew one thing for sure—George had a duty to renegotiate my contract for 1984."

Sonny's voice was soft. "Sometimes the loudest applause are the ones you never hear."

Act 54: The Negotiations

"So, George was negotiating your contract, correct?" Sonny asked.

Jervin nodded, a grin tugging at the corner of his mouth.

"Believe it or not, I was making forty grand in 1983. Players today get more than that in one at-bat. But back then? That was real money to me. George worked his magic and got me a ten-thousand-dollar raise for '84. So—fifty thousand dollars. At the time, I felt like I was making it."

He leaned back, eyes glinting with memory.

"I mean I came from nothing. I was making more money than my father ever did, by a wide margin. I was twenty-one years old and I was making moves."

He paused, then smiled wider.

"But my real windfall came with BIC INK. Our branding was catching fire. I was wearing our batting gloves, custom-made baseball gloves. A few major leaguers knew rappers, and they liked some of the designs. Started wearing them in music videos."

He chuckled.

"We'd started a catalog, too. Distributed it with deliveries, stocked in the store. Then the orders started coming in from all over the country. We had to hire more people just to keep up."

He shook his head, still amazed.

"One day, I'm watching MTV, and there it is—our gear. Then I saw it again in *Jet Magazine*. That kind of exposure? It caught the eye of a major merchandise company. They were big in sneakers, but they wanted to expand—and we were doing exactly what they were looking for."

He leaned forward, voice lowering.

"They approached us. They wanted to buy our merchandise, the patent—that was the key—and they wanted our design artist as part of the deal. They offered five million dollars."

Jervin laughed.

"George told them, 'We'll get back to you.' I was thinking, *Does George know what he's doing?* Then he says, 'If they're willing to offer five, maybe we can get five and a half.' I thought it was risky."

He paused, savoring the memory.

"But a week and a half later, George's instincts were dead on. 'Kid,' he said, 'we have a deal. I got you all five-point-seven-five-million dollars.'"

Jervin whistled.

"I sat down and started doing the math. 'Okay, that's $862,500 for you. And $1,629,333 for Rafael, Junior, and me, right?' I asked. George just nodded. 'That's about right. I trust your math.'"

He shook his head, still stunned.

"The thought of that kind of money? It was mind-boggling. I couldn't believe I was about to become a millionaire."

He smiled.

"I got invited to a party—ballplayers, celebrities, businesspeople, all kinds of people. And now, this added bonus? It made everything feel even more special."

Sonny grinned. "From the projects to patent deals. That's one hell of a negotiation."

Act 55: The Mansion

"So, tell us about this party," Sonny said.

Jervin leaned back, a grin tugging at his lips.

"Before the party, Rafael, Junior, and I went shopping. New suits. Fresh Italian shoes. Cologne that smelled like ambition. We had to look the part—hell, we were in a different tax bracket now. Junior always said, 'You got to look the part.' That night, we looked like we wrote the script."

He chuckled.

"We pulled up to this beautiful white mansion in the Hamptons, dressed like kings—designer blazers, crisp shirts, tailored pants, and shoes that clicked like confidence on marble floors. Sunglasses on, even though it was early December. Silent, but dangerous."

He paused, remembering.

"Rafael looked like my bodyguard—six-four, two-forty-five, with a streak of premature gray slicing through his hair and a beard groomed like a runway model. Junior? He looked like a reggaeton star before reggaeton was even a thing. That Daddy Yankee energy—rough, magnetic. He had that look since we were kids. The kind that made people cross the street."

Jervin smiled.

"I had my hair slicked back, looking like a goodfella. People used to tease me, said I had whiteboy hair. I wore it like armor. And all of us? We wore our BIC INK gold chains. It was a reminder of how we got here."

They stepped into the mansion.

"Workers greeted us at the door. The speakers were booming—Madonna's 'Holiday' thumped through the walls. They led us into what I guessed was the living room.

Or a ballroom. Hell, it was my first time in a mansion—what did I know?"

He shook his head.

"Inside, women floated by in outfits that defied gravity. Alcohol flowed like water. Celebrities mingled with athletes, movie stars, and the kind of rich folks you never see on TV. It was an underground society. No cameras. No paparazzi. Just power and pleasure."

A beat.

"A major leaguer approached me and said he'd introduce me around. I nodded but didn't move. I didn't understand this world. I didn't trust it."

He leaned forward, voice lowering.

"We were handed beers. Offered hors d'oeuvres. Rafael scanned the room, then froze. 'Oh shit,' he said. 'These motherfuckers got bowls of blow. Look at that! They're sniffing like there's no tomorrow.'"

The music shifted—house music. Strobe lights pulsated. The room spun. Laughter echoed. Women raised their voices to compete with the chaos.

"I felt dizzy. Uncomfortable. I stepped outside. The air hit differently. Cold, but clean. Better than that debacle inside."

He looked up, as if seeing the stars again.

"Junior and Rafael followed me out. Junior…Rafael,' I said, 'Let's get the fuck out of here.'"

"'What's wrong, Jervin?' Junior asked."

"I pointed back at the mansion. 'This shit right here? It's a trap. I'll fuck up my career. I want to leave.'"

He paused.

"They looked disappointed. I felt bad. They wanted to party. I told them, 'You guys can stay. I understand. I'm sorry. A party's a party. But this? This isn't for me. Just be careful.'"

They shook hands. Jervin walked to his car, started the engine, let it purr, and pulled away from the mansion.

"The radio came on. 'Brass in Pocket' by The Pretenders. That song reminded me of Anna. She loved that song. But the thought only lasted a millisecond."

He looked at Sonny.

"I remember what Rafael once told me, 'Know when to swing. Know when to walk away.' I did both tonight."

Sonny nodded. "You didn't just walk out of the party. You walked into your purpose."

Act 56: The Envelope

"So, what was the next chapter in your agenda?" Sonny asked.

Jervin leaned forward, his voice low and steady.

"George and I were sitting in my condo, sipping coffee, talking about my parents. Out of nowhere, I said, 'I want to help them.'"

He paused, remembering.

"George put his cup down and looked at me. 'I'm listening,' he said.

'I want to give them money for a down payment on a house. Get them out of the projects.'

George nodded. 'I'll help you.'

They drove to the Lower East Side in George's brand-new car—leather seats, a dashboard that looked like it belonged in a spaceship.

"I remember thinking, Damn, I'm making this motherfucker rich."

As they pulled up to the building, Jervin turned to him.

"Stay in the car. Make sure you lock it." I pulled out a .38 and slid it into the glove compartment.

George blinked. 'Why are you carrying that?'

'George,' I said, 'this city's got a lot of crime. I have no plans of being a victim. Now put it in the glove box. If any of these motherfuckers approach the car, don't be shy to use it.'

He looked at me like I'd just grown a second head.

'I mean, my father doesn't really know you,' I added. 'And he's always been suspicious of outsiders. No offense.'"

Jervin stepped out and approached the building. The memories hit him like a wave.

"The lobby still reeked of piss. Someone was frying chicken on the ground floor, and somehow, that smell was fighting the piss for dominance. The same scratched-up plexiglass window in the lobby. French fries and chicken wings scattered near the stairwell like a takeout bag exploded. Same old shit. Different year."

He took the elevator—sixteen floors up.

"I always hated elevators. But the view from the kitchen window? You could see the antenna of the Empire State Building. That was my escape as a kid."

He reached the sixteenth floor.

"I walked to the door. No idea how they'd react. It'd been almost three years. I knocked. I heard the shuffle of slippers. Then his voice. 'Who is it?' As he looked through the peephole.

Jesus, dude, I thought to myself. Are you serious?

'It's me, Jervin.'

The door opened halfway.

'Can I come in?' I asked.

He looked at me like I was a Jehovah's Witness interrupting his Sunday coffee. Finally, he let me in. Didn't ask how I was. Just said, 'What happened?'

Classic."

Jervin sat at the old Formica table, the same one from when he was five. Same set. Same spot where his father used to curse at the world and call everything a racket.

"I gestured for him to sit. He did. We sat in silence. Then I said, 'I've been thinking. You folks have worked hard your whole lives.'"

His mother entered, smiling. He stood and hugged her. She beamed. She opened her mouth to speak, but his father waved her to be quiet. She stood behind his chair.

"It's time for you to have your own home," I said.

I reached into my coat, pulled out an envelope, and slid it across the table.

"My father looked at it, then at me. Then he passed it to my mother.

'I don't have my glasses,' he muttered.

'How's your diabetes?' I asked.

'I need insulin every morning.'

'You inject yourself?'

'Yes.'"

His mother opened the envelope. Her eyes widened.

"This is a lot of money," she said.

'It's okay, Ma. I want you to buy a house. Have a better life.'

My father looked away. Hand on his chin. Eyes glassy.

'I have a lawyer—my agent. He'll help with the paperwork. All the particulars.' I tried to lighten the moment. 'I mean I pay him enough. That's the least he can do for me.'"

My father smiled, I think. Maybe.

My mother hugged me. My father wasn't a hugger, so I tapped him on the shoulder.

'Keep watching the games,' I said. 'I'm starting at short this year.'

Outside, George was still in the car, playing music. Jervin tapped on the window. George jumped, hand twitching toward the glove box—then relaxed.

'Open the door,' I said.

I slammed it shut behind me.

'Why do you always slam the door?' George asked.

'Sorry. Didn't realize how light it was.'

'So…how'd it go?'

'Better than I expected. I think my father's going to need a doctor. Quite sure he sprained a facial muscle. I could swear he smiled.'

George laughed.

'What are you listening to?' I asked.

'Classical music.'

'I know it's classical. But you're in the hood. I'd rather hear Run DMC, but that's just me.'

'Figures,' George said.

'Okay, George. Take me home—with your elevator music.'

They pulled away from the curb. Jervin looked back at the building.

"I thought about how I survived that place in the seventies. Rafael once told me, 'You don't escape the block. You rewrite it.'

That envelope? I rewrote my parents' lives."

Sonny nodded. "You didn't just give them a house. You gave them a way out. And a way back to you."

Act 57: The Dance and the Division

Sonny leaned in with a grin. "Okay, let's talk about 1984. Not the book—the season."

Jervin laughed. "Alright. I'll speak in a non-Orwellian way."

He leaned back, eyes flickering with memory.

"The offseason was wild. The Mets traded Carlos Diaz and Bob Bailor for Sid Fernandez. But the big one? They let Tom Seaver walk. That one hit differently. Seaver was a legend. But to me? He barely said a word."

Jervin shook his head.

"I remember going to the mound once. Picked up the rosin bag, tossed it to the ground. I tried to help. 'I know this kid from the minors,' I said. 'He's a pull hitter.' Seaver just stared at me. No response. I walked back to short with my tail between my legs."

He smirked.

"Then there was Keith Hernandez. One day he barked at me, 'Okay, Fred Astaire-less dancing, more accurate throws.' That was Keith. No sugar, all salt."

He sipped his drink.

"Ron Darling got called up in late September of 1983. And Dwight Gooden? He made the club out of spring training. Our paths crossed again. That kid was electric."

Jervin's face lit up.

"During spring training, I ran into Rico—my boy from Miami University. He was in the Cardinals' farm system. We hugged each other like it had been a decade. I used to call him Rico Cartel, after Rico Carty. He called me Julius Jervin, like Dr. J."

He chuckled.

"So, what've you been doing?" I asked. "Still trying to write the Puerto Rican version of *A Street Car Named Desire*," he said.

I laughed. "You serious?"

"Dead serious," he said. "It's going to be Estandly and Estella. Blanche becomes Blanca. And do you remember that Brando scene? When he rips his shirt and screams 'Stella!' Well, Estandly is going to have a guayabera instead. In my version, Estandly's going to yell, 'Mira Estella…Estella... ESTELLA!'"

He acted it out right there on the field. I was dying.

Jervin smiled, then shifted.

"I started the season at shortstop. But later, the Mets acquired Ray Knight. Hubie Brooks moved from third to short, and I got platooned with Wally Backman. When I didn't start, I'd come in late to replace Hubie. I didn't like it. But I was wet behind my ears. No leverage. Had to keep my mouth shut and play."

He paused.

"Of course, when I was with Junior and Rafael, I bitched. But those were private moments."

He leaned forward.

"We made a run for the National League East. Came up short to the Cubs. They had Ryne Sandberg—MVP that year. Rick Sutcliffe won the Cy Young. And Lee Smith? That man threw fire."

Jervin nodded.

"I was platooning with Wally, so I studied Sandberg. Smooth hands. Smart player. I had a decent season—batted .265, showed some power, some speed. Nothing flashy. But solid."

He looked up, eyes steady.

"We didn't win the East. But we won the league's respect. And Doc—Dwight Gooden—he won Rookie of the Year. Deserved it."

A beat.

"1984? That was a steppingstone. Something bigger was coming."

Act 58: Lessons from 1984

Sonny leaned forward, curiosity dancing in his eyes. "So, what did 1984 teach you?"

Jervin smirked, then grew thoughtful.

"One thing I learned that year—don't get too close to teammates. It's like going to battle. You fight together, bleed together, but you don't always come back together. One day you're laughing in the dugout, the next they're gone—traded, released, or worse, injured. Careers end in a blink. Best to keep your distance. Live for the moment."

Sonny nodded slowly, then grinned. "You were known around New York by then. Finished a full season with the Mets. Did you hit the hot spots?"

He leaned in, teasing now. "And I've heard—just speculation, of course," he chuckled, "you had your share of women. Trust me, my aunts used to call you the Boricua Papi Chulo."

Jervin burst out laughing. "Man, your aunts need to relax."

Sonny raised an eyebrow. "So? Any famous women? You don't have to name names."

Jervin leaned back, a sly smile playing on his lips.

"Well, yeah. I started hitting the scene. I had a few dollars now, a little shine. I was getting invited to the right places. Met some legends—David Bowie, Paul McCartney, Mick Jagger. I had a conversation with Madonna once. We talked about the Lower East Side. She lived there when she was starting out. Said she used to hustle gigs and crash on couches just a few blocks from where I grew up."

He paused, eyes lighting up.

"But my biggest thrill? Meeting Grandmaster Flash. That was different. That was home. That was the soundtrack of my youth. The streets, the block, the rhythm of the city— it all came rushing back when I shook his hand."

Jervin leaned back, eyes fixed on a memory only he could see.

"I was with famous pop singers—though they weren't famous at the time. Later on, yeah, they blew up. I was also involved with an actress-singer who was about twenty years older than me. We had a fling. You could say she was a cougar before that term even existed."

Sonny laughed. "I mean, you were twenty-two, had a condo, drove a nice car, played shortstop for the Mets, owned a business, and were a millionaire. You were living the dream."

Jervin nodded, but his smile faded.

"Yeah…but honestly? None of it meant much when the lights dimmed and the room went quiet,"

He paused, then leaned forward, elbows on his knees.

"One quick story. I was seeing this aspiring actress— she'd already done a couple of movies. One morning, I woke up to the smell of food. It pulled me out of a dead sleep. I walked into the kitchen, and there she was—nothing but a pair of socks and a thong, cooking me breakfast."

He shook his head, half-laughing.

"She turned, smiled, and said, 'I thought you might be hungry.' And I just stood there, thinking, damn…this beautiful woman is cooking me breakfast. It felt surreal."

He looked at Sonny, voice softening.

"You know, Rafael once told me, 'Don't chase the spotlight. Chase the light.' I was still learning the difference."

Sonny nodded, his voice low. "Funny how the crowd gets louder…but the silence at home gets deeper."

Jervin exhaled, the weight of it all settling in.

"Exactly. You can be surrounded by people, cameras, noise—and still feel like you're the only one in the room. I had everything I thought I wanted. But sometimes, I'd come home, sit on the edge of the bed, and feel like I was still that kid staring out the window on the sixteenth floor, looking for the Empire State Building."

He paused.

"Fame is loud. But peace? Peace is quiet. And I was still trying to find it."

Act 59: Negotiations 1985

"So, George had to negotiate your contract for the 1985 season," Sonny said, leaning in with interest. "Tell us about that."

Jervin gave a dry chuckle. "Well, since it was my third year of service, I still didn't have much leverage. Back then, if you didn't negotiate, the team could just set your salary. So yeah, it was better to negotiate—even if you were at their mercy."

He sipped his coffee.

"I told George, 'Try to get the best deal you can.'"

Sonny raised an eyebrow. "Did he?"

Jervin shrugged. "He did what he could. It was peanuts compared to today's salaries. George got me eighty grand for the '85 season. Not exactly life-changing, but I wasn't sweating it. My real money was coming from the business."

He leaned forward, eyes lighting up.

"Our plan was to rebrand. We'd sold the BIC INK patents, so we needed a new identity. We renamed the store Jerry's—a nod to my grandfather's name and the original owner. But also, something that felt neighborhood-rooted. Under that, we launched our new line: Jura-Class. We patented the modern designs, new materials, and new vibe. Sleek, bold, ours."

He smiled.

"We were even eyeing the store next door. Thinking about buying out the owner. Had plans for it—but that's a story for later."

Sonny grinned. "You guys were building an empire."

"Trying to," Jervin said. "For the grand opening, we wanted to make it special. I signed a hundred photos—five bucks a pop. But I wanted to make it more than just a money grab. So, I called up Rico. Got him to fly in and sign autographs with me. It was a promotion, but it was also a statement: we were keeping the store in the neighborhood. It was becoming iconic. I was a ballplayer now, but I was still from there."

He paused, then added, "Of course, we needed security. Luckily, Junior had two brothers in law enforcement. Raymond was with the FBI. Robert was NYPD. So, we were covered."

Sonny nodded. "Sounds like you had a solid plan. But what about the Mets? From what I've read, most teams were paying more."

Jervin's smile thinned.

"The Mets weren't the Yankees. Yankees paid their guys. The Mets? They were frugal. Always trying to get a bang for their buck. But they had Frank Cashen. That man was a baseball genius. He was building something. You could feel it."

He paused, then added, "I always go back to what Rafael told me: 'Don't wait for them to pay you. Build something they can't ignore.' Jura-Class and Jerry's—that was going to be that."

Sonny leaned back, impressed. "You didn't just play the game. You learned how to play the system."

Jervin nodded. "Exactly. And once you learn the system, you stop waiting for permission."

Act 60: Bellmore Snowfall

Over the holidays, I visited my parents' new home in Bellmore, Long Island. For the first time I could remember, they looked happy. Not just content, but genuinely happy. My mother had a brand-new kitchen, and she moved through it like it was a ballroom. She hummed while she cooked, and even my father—stoic, stubborn, old-school—was helping her. It was like the house had breathed new life into them.

As we sat at the table, my father looked up from his plate.
"Did you hear the Mets traded for Gary Carter?"

I blinked. "What?"

"They just announced it on the radio. What's the matter, you don't have a radio in your car?"

I was sitting on the couch, but got up and turned on the TV. There it was—Gary Carter, now a Met. I stood there, stunned. I was going to be playing with a legend. That trade told me everything I needed to know: the Mets were serious about winning.

But then came the gut punch.

"Looks like Hubie Brooks was part of the deal," my father added.

I sat back down, quiet. I liked Hubie. Talented player and a good guy. It all made sense now—why they'd moved him to shortstop. They were displaying him. Making him marketable. And it came at my expense.

My father cleared his throat. "They also traded for Howard Johnson."

Then, deadpan: "Is that the ice cream or the hotel?"

I laughed out loud. My father—the man I used to joke had his funny bone surgically removed—was cracking jokes. Bellmore really had changed him.

After dinner, my mother brought out her famous Spanish coffee. That stuff was so strong, I used to joke that if you poured it into a dying plant, it would spring back to life. I sipped it slowly, careful not to get the shakes. Their chihuahua sat by the radiator, trembling like he'd seen a ghost. I half-joked to myself that my mother had been sneaking him sips of her coffee. That would explain a lot.

My father and I sat in the living room. To my left, a sliding glass door looked out onto the backyard. I stared through it for a while, and then—softly, silently—it began to snow.

I stood, pulled on my coat, and stepped outside. The backyard was still. An evergreen tree stood tall in the corner, and the snow settled on its branches like nature was decorating by hand. It looked magical. Peaceful. Like something out of a dream.

After a few minutes, I went back inside. I settled onto the couch, and my father moved closer. He picked up the remote, turned down the TV, and looked at me.

"Listen," he said. "If I'm ever in a situation where these miserable doctors want to put me on life support or jam tubes down my throat—tell them to pull the plug."

He took a sip of coffee. "Your mother…she's not strong enough to make that decision."

Then he reached out, putting his finger on my chest. "But I know you are."

I nodded. I didn't say anything. I didn't need to. When a man asks you to carry his dignity, you give respect.

He looked me in the eye. "Come with me to my next appointment. Sign the proxy."

It was a morbid conversation. But it was practical, direct, and realistic. And at that moment, I saw something I hadn't seen before. We shared the same values. The same clarity. The same quiet strength.

I realized: I am his son.

For once, my father peeled back a layer of his armor. Just enough to let me see inside. Just enough to show me the vault he kept locked for decades.

Sonny leaned back in his chair, his voice soft. "Snow falls quiet…just like the moment."

Act 61: The Rafael

"So," Sonny said, leaning forward with a grin, "let's get into the '85 season."

I smiled, the memory already warming me.

"Well, before heading to Spring Training, I traded in my old ride and picked up a 1985 red Ford Mustang XL. Flashier. Louder. But I felt like I was finally driving the part. A long way from my beat-up Cutlass Supreme—or as Junior referred to it, 'my grandpa car.'"

I chuckled, remembering the way Junior used to clown me for that thing. "Man, you look like you're driving to bingo," he once said.

"Before I flew to Florida, I made a stop to see Rafael. He had a new girlfriend—Juanita. Cute Dominican girl with a soft lisp, beautiful brown hair, light brown eyes. But don't let the looks fool you—she was sharp. Binghamton grad, bachelor's in accounting, certified and everything."

I paused, shaking my head with a grin.

"Rafael was throwing an engagement party. He was planning to marry her in the fall. And let me tell you, I'd never seen him that happy. He was working the room like a politician—smiling, laughing, glowing. Juanita brought out something in him—something I didn't even know was missing until I saw it come alive."

I leaned back, remembering the moment.

"She was so good at what she did, we fired our old accountant and hired her. Replaced some bald-headed, middle-aged guy who thought sarcasm was a personality trait. I don't like firing people, but this one…I didn't lose a wink of sleep."

I watched Rafael from across the room that night, a drink in his hand, his arm around Juanita's waist. He looked like a man who had finally found his rhythm.

"I remember him telling me once, 'You know, my parents named me after the famous artist, Rafael.' And I believed him. There was something about the way he carried himself—like he was always painting his own masterpiece."

Before I left, I pulled them aside for a quick goodbye.

I turned to Juanita with a grin. "Remember—keep him out of the light. Don't get him wet. And whatever you do, never, ever feed him after midnight."

She laughed. "What is he, a gremlin?"

I pointed to the streak of premature white in Rafael's hair. "White line. White line," using the gremlin's voice.

We all laughed. I hugged them both.

"I'll see you guys in April," I said.

As I walked out, I glanced back once more. Rafael was still smiling, still glowing.

Sonny nodded, his voice soft. "Interesting that Juanita turned on the lights in Rafael's eyes. That's poetic."

I smiled. "Yeah. She didn't just turn them on—she made them dance."

Act 62: Spring of 1985

Spring Training felt different that year. The team was shifting. Fresh faces. New energy. Besides Carter and Johnson, there was Roger McDowell, Rick Aguilera, and of course—my psycho, Lenny Dykstra. Nails played every game like it was his last. I used to joke that he needed a crash helmet just to play center field. The guy had no brakes.

A few games in, I got summoned to the manager's office. My stomach dropped. I thought I was getting traded. Or released. Or demoted. That's how it usually goes—no warning. Just a knock on the door and a quiet, "Skip wants to see you."

I walked in, heart thudding.

The manager looked up. "I got a phone call from your friend. Junior."

"Really?" I said, surprised. "What did he say?"

"Here's a note. Said to call him at this number."

He handed me a slip of paper.

"Thanks, Skip," I said, already turning.

I found an office phone and dialed. It rang twice.

Then—"Yo."

"Junior, what's going on?"

His voice was tight. "Jervin…it's about Maria and Eddie."

Maria was Junior's sister. Eddie, her husband. Carolyn's parents.

"Carolyn was celebrating her birthday," he said. "Afterward, they dropped her and the other two kids off with us. They were going to dinner. A car ran a red light. Hit them."

I felt my chest tighten. "Are they okay?"

"No…" His voice cracked. "They both died."

Silence.

I closed my eyes. My heart sank. Poor Carolyn. She was just a kid. Her sister was three. Her brother, two. How do you explain that to them?

"I'm going to ask the team for time off," I said.

Junior cut me off. "That's not necessary. We got it."

"Let me worry about it," I said. "I'll be there."

The Mets gave me seven days. Told me not to worry about pay—it was Spring Training. I packed a bag and flew back to New York.

The wake was quiet. Heavy. I sat next to Carolyn, who looked smaller than I remembered. I put my arm around her. She leaned her head on my shoulder.

"How do you feel, sweetheart?" I asked.

She sighed. Didn't answer.

After a few minutes, she looked up at me. "How's your friend?"

"What friend?" I asked.

"Your pop star friend. I read magazines, you know."

I smiled. I didn't know what to say. I just held her a little closer.

Junior told me his mother and brothers would take care of the kids. They had a plan. They'd figure it out.

After the funeral, I flew back to Florida. The sun was hot, the grass was sharp, and the crack of the bat echoed like a gunshot. I played through the rest of Spring Training with Junior's voice in my head. With Carolyn's sigh in my chest.

I had a season to think about.

And 1985 was going to be one hell of a year.

Act 63: Pond Scum and Shadows

"Rafael once told me, 'The higher you climb, the colder the wind.'"

I was starting to feel the chill.

1985 was shaping up to be a dream. We were in a dogfight with the St. Louis Cardinals for the NL East. Dwight Gooden was pitching like a man possessed—every fifth day felt like a holiday, an event. Watching him work was like watching a comet streak across the sky. You didn't blink. You didn't breathe. You just watched.

And then there was the nickname.

"Pond scum," Sonny said, grinning.

"Yeah," I laughed. "Cardinal fans started calling us that. Some reporter asked me what I thought. I told him, 'I've been called worse.'"

I was having the best year of my career. I cracked my 500th hit. A quiet milestone, but it meant something to me. Every one of those hits had a story—some sweet, some bitter, all earned.

After the All-Star break, it was a dead heat. Us and the Cards, neck and neck. Every game felt like a playoff. Then, out of nowhere, the league shut down. August 6th. A strike. It only lasted two days, but it was strange—two days off in the middle of a pennant race. Like the baseball gods hit pause.

But then…Pittsburgh happened.

Sonny leaned in. "Pittsburgh, huh? That sounds like a storm."

I nodded. "That September gave Major League Baseball a black eye."

The Pittsburgh drug trials exploded like a grenade in the middle of the season. Testimonies, grand juries, headlines. Cocaine. Clubhouses. Hotel rooms. Names—big names—were dragged into the light: Keith Hernandez, Tim Raines, Dave Parker, Vida Blue, even the Pirate Parrot. Players admitted to using drugs during games, buying drugs in stadium bathrooms, stashing vials in their uniforms.

It was surreal. The league was in damage control. Commissioner Ueberroth was scrambling to save face. Suspensions were handed out, then commuted. Fines. Drug testing. Community service. But the damage was done. The public saw behind the curtain—and it wasn't pretty.

For us players, it was a gut check. The whispers in the locker room got louder. Trust got thinner. You didn't know who was clean, who was lying, who was next. The game felt different. Tainted.

And yet, we still had a season to finish. A race to run. A dream to chase.

But the chill Rafael warned me about? It was here. And it was real.

Act 64: The Babysitter Dream

"So," Sonny said, leaning forward, "'you mentioned something about a dream. What was it?"

I exhaled slowly, the memory still fresh in my mind.

"After the scandal broke, I was drained. Not physically—psychologically. I'd lie in bed at night, staring at the ceiling of my condo, trying to make sense of everything. One night, I drifted into this…strange dream. It took me back to something I hadn't thought about in years."

I paused, letting the memory settle.

"When I was four, before I even started kindergarten, my parents hired a babysitter named Iris. She lived next door. My mother trusted her—she had to. Both my parents worked, and Iris had kids of her own. A daughter a few years older than me, a teenage son about to graduate, and an older son who was a heroin addict."

Sonny raised an eyebrow but didn't interrupt.

"I remember the younger son telling me he was going to Vietnam. This was 1966. Iris used to watch Let's Make a Deal with Monty Hall and The Price Is Right with Bob Barker. Those were her shows. I didn't know what heroin was back then—not until I was ten. While other kids were playing with G.I. Joes, I was learning about life and death."

I rubbed my hands together, as if trying to warm them from the chill of the past.

"One day, Iris slipped in the shower. Hit her head. My mom told her to go to the hospital, but Iris brushed it off. Said it was just a bump. Six months later, she died of an aneurysm. She was in her late thirties."

I looked down, remembering the church.

"I went to the funeral. The wake was held in this old church. I remember the smell—incense mixed with stale air.

The stained-glass windows, the dim lights, the statues of saints watching from the shadows. The adults were worried I'd be traumatized. I was just a kid, standing on the pew, my mother holding me so I wouldn't fall into the coffin."

I looked at Sonny.

"I remember looking at Iris. She looked peaceful. I turned to my mother and said, 'She looks like she's asleep.' I didn't understand death. So I asked, 'Where do you go after you die? Am I going to die?'"

Sonny's face softened.

"My mother, in that calm, steady voice of hers, said, 'We all die at one point. Then we go to heaven so we can rest.' I asked her, 'Do you think Iris is resting now? Is she in peace?' And somehow, she made it all feel okay. Even death."

I leaned back, eyes on the ceiling again.

"In the dream, I was back in the church. I turned to the coffin, and I saw Iris being lifted—like her body was rising, floating away, carried by something I couldn't see. I woke up in a cold sweat. Couldn't shake it. I didn't know why that memory came back. It was everything that had happened—the scandal, the pressure, the grief. It was all catching up to me."

Sonny nodded slowly. "A lot of trauma from childhood finds its way into dreams. Sounds like you were going through a storm."

"Yeah," I said. "Honestly, I was just looking forward to whatever came at the end of the 1985 season. I needed the offseason. I needed to breathe."

Act 65: 98 Wins, Nothing and More

Sonny leaned in, curious. "It's September. Tell me what happened next."

I exhaled slowly. "After the trial, we went to St. Louis. Of all places, of course."

I could still hear the boos.

"Keith Hernandez got mercilessly booed by the same fans who once cheered him as a champion in 1982. I used to think Whitey Herzog traded Keith to the Mets as punishment. After all, we weren't exactly contenders in 1983. But what Herzog didn't realize was that Keith Hernandez was the biggest gift the Mets ever received."

I paused, letting the weight of the truth settle.

"We didn't care what was said or written. Hernandez and Carter were our leaders. Period. Everyone's got demons and secrets—I never judged anyone for those. I judged on performance. And in 1985, those secrets spilled. Became a spectacle. But we kept playing."

I looked at Sonny. "Rafael once told me, 'Everyone's got ghosts. The trick is learning how to play with them in the room.'"

Sonny nodded. "Tell us about the rivalry."

"The season came down to a three-game series against St. Louis in late September. We were two games back. Everything was on the line."

I could still feel the tension in the air.

"Game one, Darryl Strawberry hit an absolute bomb. Might've been off Ken Dayley. I still remember the sound— the crack of the bat, the half-second of silence, and then the dugout exploding."

I smiled.

"Game two, Howard Johnson took Todd Worrell deep. Crushed it. Whitey Herzog wasn't having it—had the bat sent to the league to check for cork. That's how hard it was hit. That's how desperate it got."

I shook my head.

"We lost game three. Just like that, St. Louis took a two-game lead with four to play. The gods weren't with us. They won the division. Beat the Dodgers in the NLCS."

I looked down.

"Ninety-eight wins. Nothing to show."

"In today's game, we'd have been a wild card. But that was a different era. One division winner. No second chances."

Sonny stayed quiet, letting me go on.

"There was a positive aspect. Dwight Gooden won the Cy Young. Best pitcher in baseball, hands down. And I had a good year—career-high 150 hits. My development was finally clicking."

I leaned back, remembering.

"When the Cardinals made the World Series, we all gathered at my place—Junior, Rafael, Juanita. Game six. The ump blew the call at first. No video review back then. Royals walked it off. Forced a Game 7."

I smiled.

"We loaded up—chips, beer, food. I didn't drink, but Rafael and Junior liked their beer. Me? I was addicted to Coca-Cola and Doritos."

I laughed softly.

"When the Royals crushed the Cardinals in Game 7, I jumped up and yelled, 'Holy shit! Did the Royals just beat the shit out of the Cardinals?' I didn't even clap. I just stared at the screen. Watching someone else celebrate… it's like looking into a mirror you don't want to see. I've been there. I've done that."

I paused.

"Rafael slapped my chest and said, 'The scoreboard lies. But the heart doesn't.'"

That night, I felt both.

Win or lose, I'd lived both sides.

Then I saw him—Lonnie Smith. Again.

I turned to Rafael. "That's the luckiest motherfucker alive."

Rafael laughed. "Third ring," he said.

I hadn't even smelled the postseason. Lonnie had been traded, released, bounced around—and there he was, on top again.

I wasn't bitter. But it didn't seem fair.

Sonny nodded slowly. "Ninety-eight wins and nothing to show. That's the kind of season that stays with you."

I looked at him, eyes steady. "Yeah. It never really leaves."

Act 66: The Handwriting

"The handwriting is on the wall," Sonny said, flipping through his notes. "What did you mean by that?"

I leaned back, eyes narrowing. "Well...the 1985 season brought hope. We came close—too close. And the offseason moves? Tim Teufel. Bobby Ojeda. The press called them the final pieces of the puzzle. Radio guys wouldn't shut up about the ninety-eight wins and missed opportunities. Most of them couldn't hit a curveball if their lives depended on it."

I paused, remembering the shift in tone that winter.

"But then the Challenger exploded. January 28th. Everything stopped. The baseball chatter faded. That was a real tragedy. Seven astronauts gone in an instant. It reminded me that we're just entertainers. That's all we are, really. In the grand scheme, we're background noise."

I looked down at my hands.

"For me, the offseason was different. I was eligible for arbitration. I didn't want it to go that far. I'd heard stories—how brutal it could be. You sit there while your own team's rep tells the arbitrator you're a glorified benchwarmer. That you're overpaid. That you should be grateful just to wear the uniform. Meanwhile, you're sitting there, muttering 'fuck you' under your breath."

I smiled faintly. "Luckily, I had George."

"George?" Sonny asked.

"My pitbull. My Roy Cohn. Nice guy, but a killer in negotiations. Lower East Side instincts. He told me, 'I'm going to ask for $250K.' I looked at him like he was crazy. 'You think they'll bite?' I asked. He smirked. 'Nah. But it's a starting point. Realistic goal is $175K.'"

I waited outside the room while George went to work. When he came out, he was grinning.

"Kid," he said, "I just got you $200K."

I laughed. "George always performed. Of course, his cut was $30K, but I didn't care. I was finally getting paid what I was worth. New tax bracket and all."

George offered to drive me home. It was a quiet ride. Halfway across the bridge, he broke the silence.

"'I got married in September,' he said."

I turned to him. "'Really? Congrats, I guess. What's her name?'"

"'Shaquanda. She's a recovering crackhead. But she's getting better now.'"

I stared at him, stunned. Gave him a look like he'd just shit himself.

"'Are you fucking crazy?' I barked."

He let me vent for a minute, then waited until we hit a red light. He turned to me, deadpan.

"'Relax. I'm just fucking with you. Her name's Venus Jackson. She's a lawyer.'"

I burst out laughing. George turned up the radio— David Bowie's *Let's Dance* was playing. I exhaled, finally relaxing.

"'She practice the same kind of law as you?' I asked."

"'Nah. She's a criminal lawyer. And yes, she's Black. Or as you say, a Sistah.'"

"'I don't say shit like that,' I shot back."

"'Yeah, yeah. I listen to the lyrics of your rap music,' he teased."

I laughed again. Truth was, I was happy for him. If anyone needed to get laid, it was George.

The Culture Club came on the radio. George turned serious.

"'Time,' he said. 'I like that song.'"

He turned the volume down. "'Speaking of time…word is—unverified—but word is the owners are colluding. Trying to keep salaries down. Kill the free agency market. We're planning to sue.'"

I sat with that for a minute. My dream was baseball. But behind the scenes? It was a shit show.

George kept going. "'And don't be surprised if they drop the roster to 24 next year.'"

I nodded quietly.

Rafael's voice echoed in my head: *Don't just read the writing. Rewrite it.*

Down in Double-A, there was a shortstop named Kevin Elster. Young. Slick glove. Cheaper. Hungrier. He was coming. I could feel it.

With my salary bump and free agency looming after '87, I knew what was coming.

The handwriting was on the wall.

I was a piece of the puzzle—but only for 1986.

After that? Who knew.

Act 67: Packing and Shadows

"So, it's 1986," Sonny said, leaning forward. "Tell us about Spring Training."

I nodded, the memory already unfolding.

"Before camp, Junior's mother called me. Said Carolyn was acting up."

"'What do you want me to do?' I asked."

"'Can she stay with you a couple of days?'"

"'I've got about a week left before I head out. She can stay the weekend.'"

Carolyn was struggling. Fourteen next month, but carrying grief like a grown woman. That weekend, I took her to see *Back to the Future*. Funny thing is, I enjoyed it as much as she did. For a couple of hours, we both got to forget.

After the movie, she wanted Red Lobster in Times Square, and then Playland for video games. We didn't stay long—people were starting to recognize me, even though I dressed down. Fame has a way of finding you, even when you're trying to hide.

Later, we sat on a bench near my place. It was February, but not freezing. The kind of day where the cold just brushes your skin instead of biting it.

"'What's wrong, kid?' I asked."

She looked at me sideways. "'I'm going to be fourteen next month. I'm hardly a kid.'"

I smiled. "'Sorry, sweetheart. It's a term of endearment.'"

"'Like the movie?' she teased."

"'Well…neither one of us is dying of cancer.'"

She smiled, then leaned in and gave me a hug. I held her close. I really loved that kid. Sweet, smart, hurting. She missed her parents. Who wouldn't?

When she left, I turned my attention to Spring Training. February 1986. I packed socks, cleats, gloves—the usual. But there was hope in every fold. I packed a few pieces from Jura-Class, hoping to get them seen. Spring Training was more relaxed about gear. I figured if I could wear it, someone would notice. We'd catch lightning again, like we did with BIC INK.

Then the phone rang.

It was Rafael.

"'What's going on? Everything okay?'"

"'No,' he said. His voice was tight. 'The FBI was here. Asking questions.'"

I froze.

"'Remember that party in 1983? The one you left early?'"

"'Yeah. What about it?'"

He exhaled. "'Turns out there were undercover agents there. Posing as businesspeople. You were smart. It was a trap. I told them you left early.'"

I didn't know what to say. I hung up and stared at my cleats. Clean. Untouched. But the world around them wasn't.

A few weeks later, the IRS came knocking. An audit. Juanita—four months pregnant and now our accountant—handled it. They were fishing. Looking for improprieties that didn't exist. But they weren't really after numbers. They were after me. A ballplayer from a neighborhood with too many drug dealers and too few chances.

Rafael once told me, "The smart ones leave early. The lucky ones don't get caught."

I was starting to understand the difference.

I looked out the window of my condo. The Manhattan skyline shimmered in the morning light. Snow was melting into slush. The sun was rising over Central Park like it had something to prove.

This was supposed to be the year. The year I could finally smell the postseason.

Spring Training was waiting.

So was the press.

And Kevin Elster.

And once again, I had to prove that I belonged.

Sonny shook his head. "Funny how seasons start with packing. And sometimes, you're packing more than gear."

Act 68: Spring in Florida 1986

"So, it's 1986," Sonny said. "You've got all three external factors swirling around. What's running through your mind?"

I leaned back, eyes narrowing as the memory came into focus.

"Florida was a ray of sunshine—literally. After everything in New York, it felt like a relief. The noise, the press, the tension—it was all adding pressure. I needed a reset. Spring Training gave me that. The sun hit differently down there. The air felt lighter. The mornings were quiet— just the sound of cleats crunching gravel, gloves popping, players stretching, the low hum of batting practice. And hope. Always that low hum of hope."

I looked around camp and saw the future. Prospects, like I once was. Talent everywhere. George Foster was still a force, even if he kept to himself. Mookie Wilson—steady, smooth, no drama. A pro's pro. My little psycho, Lenny Dykstra, played like his hair was on fire. No brakes. No fear. Fans loved him. He was becoming a star.

Darryl Strawberry? Long, lean, lethal. A machine. The Mets were lucky to have him. And Big Kevin Mitchell—man, he was the ultimate gamer. He could hit, run, fight, and laugh all in one inning. Danny Heep? The kind of guy who'd win you a game and disappear before the cameras showed up. No flash. Just clutch.

Dances with the Dirt

It was a loaded team. And I was part of it.

But I knew the clock was ticking.

Kevin Elster was in my shadow. A September call-up waiting to happen. The press circled like vultures. This spring, I had to prove again that I wasn't just a veteran presence—I was still a force.

Ray Knight and Howard Johnson were set to platoon at third. Wally Backman and Tim Teufel at second. And at first? The expert himself—Keith Hernandez. Best first baseman of my generation. Behind the plate, Gary Carter. Future Hall of Famer. Ed Hearn backing him up.

The pitching? Outstanding.

Dwight Gooden, fresh off his Cy Young. Ron Darling, the best number two in the game. Sid Fernandez, the hard-throwing lefty repping Hawaii with number 50. Bobby Ojeda, the new lefty with an edge Frank Cashen called "an intangible." Rick Aguilera—underrated, versatile, valuable.

In the bullpen, we had two closers. Roger McDowell, the prankster—loved giving hot feet. And Jesse Orosco, the veteran lefty we got for Jerry Koosman. Doug Sisk had fallen out of favor with the fans, which was a shame. Once you lose Mets fans, it's hard to get them back. They could be brutal.

Sonny cut in. "Quick—worst fan base?"

I didn't hesitate. "Phillies fans. Easy. I once heard them boo Mike Schmidt. I'm like, 'How the fuck do you boo Mike Schmidt? What the fuck is wrong with these people?'"

We both laughed.

"Anyway," I continued, "we also had Randy Niemann. I had no idea who he was. Thought he was the guy who sang *Short People* and became a pitcher after his music career dried up. Turns out—not the same guy."

Halfway through camp, I was driving with the window down. *Manic Monday* by The Bangles came on the radio. That song always reminded me of New York—the subway crush, the Monday morning madness. Four years of high school packed into a sardine can. I don't know how I survived that insanity.

But I did.

And now, there was something in the air. Optimism. Real optimism. It felt different this time. Like we weren't just hoping to win—we were expected to win. And that's a dangerous kind of confidence.

I was ready to fight. To be part of a gladiator team.

And George? George was on point. When camp broke, we went north with twenty-four on the roster—not twenty-five. Something was definitely going on with the owners.

Sonny nodded. "Spring's funny. It makes you forget the weight. Until the games start counting."

I looked out the window, Florida sun pouring in.

"Yeah," I said. "And then it all comes rushing back."

Act 69: The Grind

"Tell us about the grind?" Sonny asked.

I laughed. "Well, we were off to a tremendous start—with a few fights along the way."

May was wild. George Foster hit a grand slam against the Dodgers. Next batter up? Ray Knight. The Dodgers pitcher didn't like the celebration and plunked him. Knight didn't like being plunked and charged the mound. Benches cleared. A few punches were thrown, but mostly it was baseball theatre—more peacemaking than real aggression. Still, there's always a few hotheads in the mix.

It reminded me of a street fight. Except in the streets, you never know who's packing heat. I'd had my share of those. But at this level? I'd rather talk my way out—unless I had no choice.

Two weeks later, our first base coach, Bill Robinson, got into it with a Pirates pitcher. This one wasn't theatre. Fists flew. Both benches cleared. Kevin Mitchell nearly strangled the Pirates shortstop. Ron Darling had to scream at him to let go. I might've been imagining it, but I swear the guy's lips were turning purple. Mitch had hands like cinder blocks. Later in his career, he got into it with Davey Johnson—punched him clean. Davey said it felt like getting hit with a hammer.

Mitch was a San Diego gangbanger. He was my kind of guy.

Then came July.

Right before the All-Star break, Gary Carter hit a grand slam. Next batter? Darryl Strawberry. The Braves pitcher plunked him. Not smart. Darryl—six-foot-six of fury—charged the mound like a freight train. It took half the team to hold him back before he turned the guy into a chalk outline.

And then, the surprise of my life.

I was selected as a reserve for the All-Star Game.

I almost cried when I heard. I was having a career year, sure—but I never expected to be picked. And the guy who picked me? Whitey Herzog. The same man who once traded away Keith Hernandez. Life's funny like that.

That night, I called Rafael.

"Juanita gave birth," he said, his voice full of joy. "It's a boy. We named him Rafael Jr.—RJ."

"That sounds like a winner to me," I said, smiling like an uncle. "Congratulations."

Then he added, "I just heard on the radio—you made the All-Star team. Kid, I'm so proud of you. You earned it. Congratulations."

After we hung up, I sat there staring at my All-Star gear. It wasn't just a uniform. It was proof. Proof that I belonged. That I mattered. That the road I'd walked—every cracked sidewalk, every late-night batting cage, every doubt—had led somewhere.

I got choked up. Just for a minute.

Rafael once told me, "The grind doesn't care who you are. But it'll show you who you are."

That summer, I found out who I was.

Houston was waiting.

So was the second half.

And somehow, I knew—this season was special.

By all means.

Sonny grinned. "Fists flew. Babies cried. And you? You finally got your name in lights."

Act 70: Among Legends

"Tell us about your All-Star experience," Sonny said.

I smiled, the memory still fresh in my bones.

"The All-Star Game was a whirlwind," I said. "It's an event that starts on Monday and doesn't stop until the final out Tuesday night. You're signing baseballs, doing interviews, shaking hands, posing for photos. It's nonstop."

I leaned back in my chair.

"I knew most of the National League guys. We'd played against each other, shared dugouts, swapped stories. But the American League? That was a different world. No interleague play back then—you didn't see those guys unless it was October…or July."

I paused, letting the names roll through my mind like a highlight reel.

"The American League was stacked. Eddie Murray. Jim Rice. Harold Baines. George Brett. Kirby Puckett. Rickey Henderson. Wade Boggs. Cal Ripken Jr. Dave Winfield. Don Mattingly. And Roger Clemens started the game. Young, cocky, and on top of the world."

I shook my head, still in awe.

"Over in the National League, we had our own legends. Dave Parker. Tim Raines. Tony Gwynn. Ryne Sandberg. Mike Schmidt. Ozzie Smith. And the Mets? We were well represented. Gary Carter, Keith Hernandez, and Darryl Strawberry. Strawberry got the most votes of anyone. He was a star now. A real one."

I smiled again. "Whitey Herzog picked Davey Johnson to be on his coaching staff. And starting for the National League? Dwight Gooden."

I looked at Sonny. "What a journey. From sitting next to him in 1982 as two draftees, to standing beside him in the All-Star dugout. That's a hell of a ride."

I took a breath.

"Before the game, I had one thought—if I get in and get an at-bat, it'll be the thrill of my lifetime."

And I did get in.

Not just once—twice.

"Second at-bat, I singled to left field. Asked for the ball. They gave it to me. When I got back to the dugout, I held it like it was gold. Like it was proof."

I looked down at my hands, remembering the weight of the ball

"When the game ended, I was drained. But I soaked it all in. The lights. The legends. The moment."

I paused.

"I was never a superstar. I was a lunchbox guy. Blue-collar worker, white-collar salary. But that night? I belonged."

I looked up, eyes steady.

Rafael once told me, "You don't just play among legends. You become part of the story."

And that night, I did.

Act 71: Clinched

"The All-Star Game in Houston," I told Sonny. "Lucky for us, we had a series with the Astros right after, so we didn't have to travel. I was exhausted, so I welcomed the idea of rest. The All-Star Game was one thing—but with the '86 Mets, drama always followed."

I laughed, shaking my head.

"Tim Teufel had just become a father. He was out celebrating with Ron Darling, Bobby Ojeda, and Rick Aguilera. From what I understood, a bar fight broke out. All four of them got arrested. Held for eleven hours. Posted an $800 bond and were released."

I paused, grinning.

"My twenty-four-year-old mind pictured all four of them in cowboy hats and spurs, walking into that bar like it was a saloon. I imagined Teufel slamming a shot glass down and throwing the first punch. Darling breaking a chair over someone's back. The whole thing like a Wild West brawl."

I shook my head again. "That was July."

"Then came Cincinnati. Another fight. This time, Ray Knight and Eric Davis. Davis slid hard into third, and Ray didn't like it. He punched Davis, benches cleared, and chaos erupted. I swear I saw three guys trying to hit Kevin Mitchell at once. Someone tugged on my jersey—I lost half my buttons that season."

I laughed again.

"I had already been taken out of the game earlier on a double switch. Ray Knight, Kevin Mitchell, and Darryl Strawberry were all ejected. George Foster never left the bench. Just sat there and later said, 'It wasn't my fight.'"

I leaned forward, eyes gleaming.

"So now we had no third baseman. No right fielder. Davey Johnson didn't panic. He got creative. Howard Johnson moved to short. Gary Carter—our catcher—made an emergency appearance at third. And in right field?"

I smiled wide.

"Davey made one of the most genius moves I've ever seen. He platooned Roger McDowell and Jesse Orosco. Literally. When a lefty came up, Orosco jogged in from right to pitch. When a righty stepped in, McDowell did the same. It was insane. It was brilliant. And it worked. We won."

I shook my head in disbelief. "Not even in Little League did I ever see anything like that. In 1986, Davey Johnson was living a charmed life."

I paused, letting the memory settle.

"Then came September. We clinched the division against the Cubs. A little redemption from 1984, when we won ninety games and went home. This time, we were celebrating."

I looked down, smiling.

"We were far from done—October was coming. And this time? We weren't just invited. We were ready to crash the party."

I could still hear Rafael's voice in my head: "Winning doesn't change you. It just shows you who you've been all along."

That night, it rang true.

Sonny nodded slowly. "You didn't just clinch a division. You clinched your place in history."

Act 72: RJ and the Real Ones

"Tell us about the aftermath of the celebration," Sonny said.

I leaned back, the memory still warm.

"After we clinched, I asked management for a couple of days off to handle some personal matters. Their response?

'We've got Howard Johnson, Kevin Mitchell, and we called up Kevin Elster—we'll be fine.'"

I grinned. "I caught the Elster dig. I shot back, 'Don't forget Carter.' Got a half laugh. Then I reminded them—Gary Carter wasn't just a catcher. He was a gifted athlete. A leader."

I needed to see Rafael. I needed to meet RJ.

The whole drive to Queens, my mind was on the postseason. I'd been seen by millions over the years, but this was different. The postseason was national. It was legacy. It was the biggest stage of my career.

When I pulled up to Rafael and Juanita's new place, I was struck. Juanita greeted me at the door, warm as always. I stepped inside and froze.

"Damn," I said, staring at the parquet floors. "My floors aren't even this nice."

Then I saw the marble fireplace. The whole place was immaculate. Tasteful. It looked like it belonged in a magazine. It looked like them—solid, grounded, built to last.

Juanita led me to the nursery. She lifted RJ from his bassinet and turned to me.

"You want to hold him?"

I froze.

Rafael stepped in, grinning. "Hold him, bro. Didn't the scouting report say you had soft hands?"

I laughed nervously. Then Juanita handed him to me.

I held RJ like he was made of glass. Like a Fabergé egg. It was the first time I'd ever held a baby. I cradled him gently, close to my chest. My hand found the back of his tiny neck. I rocked him, slow and soft. I caught the scent of baby oil—or whatever babies are supposed to smell like.

And then…something clicked.

It was like a switch flipped. A paternal instinct I didn't know I had. I felt a connection. A heartbeat. I looked into his eyes and saw nothing but innocence. And I felt…good. Natural. Almost magical.

Juanita and Rafael smiled. They saw it. They knew I was stepping into something new—like I'd just unlocked a part of myself I didn't know existed.

RJ started to fall asleep on my chest. It was like the rhythm of my heartbeat calmed him. I found myself whispering to him, like he could understand.

I told him things I'd never said out loud. About dreams. About fears. About how winning means nothing if you've got no one to share it with.

When RJ drifted off, Rafael leaned in and whispered, "I got your back. Juanita's got your back. We're praying and hoping you win."

"You want playoff tickets?" I asked.

Juanita smiled. "Just get two. One for Rafael, one for Junior. I'll watch it on TV. I need rest."

"Okay, girl," I said, stretching the word like a joke.

She giggled.

But I meant it. I trusted them. Rafael, Junior, Juanita—they weren't just my friends. They were my foundation. After the postseason, we'd sit down. Talk expansion. Talk vision. Because RJ wasn't just a baby.

He was the future.

George was my agent, but he was family too. He managed my career—my TV spots, my radio hits, my endorsements. Negotiated my contracts. And when you're not a superstar, you need someone who can market you like one.

George wanted to bring in a professional business manager. I told him, "Absolutely not."

I'd heard the horror stories. Players robbed blind by guys in suits with smooth talk and slick contracts. But I wasn't a carefree, clueless kid. The streets taught me how to spot the con men.

And to recognize the real ones.

Being savvy wasn't optional. It was survival.

Sonny nodded. "You held a baby. You kept a promise. And you held your ground. Now that's real."

Act 73: The Thread in the Tapestry

"Okay," Sonny said, leaning forward. "Tell us about your analysis of the 1986 Mets."

I smiled. "You want the truth? That team was a perfect storm. Grit, clutch, pitching, power, defense. We weren't just built—we were stitched together. Like a thread in a tapestry."

I leaned back, letting the memory spool out.

"George Foster fell out of favor with the brass and got released. That was a big move. In his place, we picked up Lee Mazzilli on waivers. And the irony? Mazzilli was the DNA of this club. Number one pick in 1974. He *was* the Mets in the late '70s. Then after the 1981 season, he gets traded to Texas for Ron Darling and Walt Terrell. And what does Frank Cashen do? Flips Terrell for Howard Johnson. That's how you build a contender—one thread at a time."

I could see it all so clearly.

"The key acquisitions between 1983 and 1985 were Keith Hernandez, Ray Knight, and Gary Carter. That's your spine. That's your heartbeat. And then you add Bobby Ojeda, Sid Fernandez, Tim Teufel—guys who weren't just role players. They were difference makers."

I paused, then added, "But the soul of that team? That was the homegrown talent."

I ticked them off like a roll call.

"Me. Roger McDowell. Wally Backman. Darryl Strawberry. Mookie Wilson. Rick Aguilera. Lenny Dykstra. And of course, Dwight Gooden. We weren't just teammates—we were forged in the same fire."

I leaned in.

"Then you had guys like Kevin Mitchell and Doug Sisk—undrafted, overlooked—but they fit. They belonged. That team wasn't perfect on paper. But in the clubhouse? On the field? We were a storm heading into battle."

I looked at Sonny.

"That's the 1986 Mets. A team built on trades, trust, and timing. A team that didn't just want to win—we expected to. And when you mix that kind of talent with that kind of edge?"

I smiled.

"You get history."

Act 74: Game One — Houston

"Okay," Sonny said, "it's Game One. Let's hear your thoughts."

I leaned back, eyes narrowing as the memory came into focus.

"I always looked at the Astrodome like it was an airport," I said. "That dome—it made everything feel weird, but unique. Like we were about to take off."

It was a dream matchup. Dwight Gooden, the reigning Cy Young winner, against Mike Scott, the man who'd go on to win it in 1986. I met Scott back in 1982, fresh off the draft. Gooden and I had been on this journey together since then—two kids trying to make it, now standing on the biggest stage.

But what really dazzled me wasn't the pitching duel.

It was looking across the dugout and seeing Yogi Berra in an Astros uniform.

Yogi was a Yankees legend, sure. But to me, he was a Mets legend too. He coached under Gil Hodges in 1969, then took over as manager in 1972 after Hodges died suddenly. Berra led the Mets to the 1973 World Series. That stuck with me. Still does.

But the greatest feeling—before the first pitch, before the nerves kicked in—was the lineup introduction.

As a kid, me and my brother Manny used to play make-believe. We'd mimic the Shea Stadium announcer, trying to recreate that echo.

"Leading off… leading off… the right fielder… the right fielder… Jervin… Jervin… Class… Class…"

We'd stretch it out, make it sound official. Like we were already there.

I started as a right fielder. But when I was fourteen, I joined this team and practiced every position just to stay sharp. One day, this Italian manager—Mr. Augustino— pulled me aside.

"You're gonna be my shortstop," he said in that wise-guy voice.

"But I don't play short," I told him.

"I've seen you practice. You can play short."

I hesitated. Thought about arguing. Thought about my kneecaps. Then I said, "Sure. I'm your shortstop."

Harry Albino

Best decision I ever made.

So when I heard the Astrodome announcer say, "Batting eighth, playing shortstop, Jervin Class," I smiled.

I got some claps—I'm sure it was my teammates—but I jogged out between the foul lines like I was back in the park, pretending. As the rest of the lineup was introduced, I imagined Manny in the stands, wearing his Marine uniform, staring at me with that proud, unblinking look. I could feel him during the anthem, like he was standing right behind me.

Then it was time to play ball.

Mike Scott was untouchable.

I mean, we could've brought in that tree from the Bugs Bunny cartoon and still wouldn't have hit him. The ball danced like it had a mind of its own. It was like trying to hit a ghost.

My teammates were convinced he was scuffing the ball. Carter was the first to ask the ump to check it.

Nothing. Nada.

The only run of the game—a solo shot by Glenn Davis.

That was it. 1–0 Houston.

They took Game One.

We had to regroup.

Game Two was coming.

Act 75: The Ryan Express

"Okay," Sonny said, leaning in. "Let's go to Game Two."

I grinned. "Bobby Ojeda was on the mound for us. But I wasn't going to be easy. We had to face the legendary Nolan Ryan. The Ryan Express."

I shook my head, still in awe.

"Crazy to think he was part of the 1969 Mets championship team. I saw him pitch at Shea when I was a kid. He was the guy who refused to sing *You Gotta Have Heart* on the Ed Sullivan Show. Same team as our third base coach, Buddy Harrelson."

I laughed. "I tried to switch-hit like Buddy when I was young. It didn't work out. I looked like I was swinging a broomstick underwater."

Ryan was throwing smoke early. I mean, smoke. His pitches sounded like they could break bricks. I remember sitting in the upper deck as a kid, hearing that pop when the ball hit Jerry Grote's glove—it sounded like a gunshot.

I'd face Ryan in the regular season. Always tough. But this was different. This was October.

In my first at-bat, I hit a single off him.

It was beyond my wildest dreams. My first postseason hit. I stood at first base, heart pounding, trying not to grin like a wide-eyed rookie. I was euphoric.

Next up, Bobby Ojeda tried to bunt me over. Didn't work. I got forced out at second. I thought I was safe, but there were no replays back then. You lived with the call.

Then Dykstra singled. Backman followed with another. Ojeda came around and scored. We had the early lead.

And then—of all people—Keith Hernandez stepped up and tripled. Dykstra and Backman scored. Keith stood on third, fist pumping. Strawberry followed with a deep fly to bring him home.

Just like that, we were up 4-0.

The Ryan Express? He was starting to look like a local.

Ojeda coasted. Calm, surgical. We took Game Two, tied the series, and headed back to New York.

The flight home was smooth. Quiet. Which wasn't always the case. There was that one time the plane got trashed—but that's another story. And for the second time, I vehemently denied being involved.

I laughed.

Over in the American League, the Angels and Red Sox were still battling for the pennant. But in our clubhouse, we were focused. We'd taken a punch. We'd punch back.

After the game, I remembered something Rafael once told me:

"Even legends bleed. You just gotta swing first."

Sonny nodded. "You didn't just ride the Express. You punched the ticket."

"Okay," Sonny said, grinning. "You're tied and off to Shea. Tell us about Game Three."

I leaned in, channeling my inner Sophia from *The Golden Girls*.

"Picture it. Shea Stadium. October 1986. New York was rocking. Mets fans were hungry—starving, you could say—for a championship. It had been thirteen years since Shea had seen October baseball. I was eleven the last time the Mets were in postseason. I'm sure the 7 Line was packed with people crammed in like sardines in a can."

Bob Knepper, a crafty lefty, started for Houston. Ron Darling for us. Houston jumped on Darling early—4-0 in the first two innings. Rough start. But Darling settled down, kept us in it.

Bottom of the sixth. Houston up 4-1. Two men on. Darryl Strawberry stepped in. Knepper tried to sneak a fastball past him.

Bad idea.

Strawberry launched it into the second deck, right field porch, just above the mini scoreboard. A three-run bomb. The game was tied.

The Shea faithful erupted. The dugout exploded. I didn't just hear it—I felt it. Feet stomping. Concrete shaking. I thought the stadium might collapse. It was like a living, breathing thing. The fans were euphoric. Hungry. And so was I.

Rick Aguilera entered the game in the sixth in place of Ron Darling and promptly gave up a run. Houston took a 5-4 lead. Seventh inning, and it felt like the game was slipping away. The bats were quiet.

In the eighth, Davey Johnson brought in Jesse Orosco. Houston countered with Charlie Kerfeld.

Now listen—if Kerfeld wasn't in a Houston uniform, I'd swear he was a Yeti with glasses. Big dude. Wild hair. But he could throw. Had flair. Smooth. Likeable, even if he was trying to shut us down.

Gary Carter hit a rocket back onto the mound. Kerfeld snagged it behind his back. Showed off a little. I couldn't even get mad.

Bottom of the ninth. Still 5-4, Houston. Orosco had been solid. Now it was Dave Smith's turn to close it out for the Astros.

Wally Backman led off as a pinch hitter. Gritty. Scrappy. Hardnosed. He laid down a bunt and beat Glenn Davis to the bag. Davis missed the tag. Houston screamed that Backman ran out of the baseline. No replays back then. The umps huddled. Call stood.

Then Davey sent up Danny Heep to pinch-hit for me. Veteran lefty. I wasn't mad. I wanted to win. Ego had to sit this one out.

Heep flied out. One down.

Next up—Lenny Dykstra.

Lenny, with his usual wad of chewing tobacco, stepped in. Took a hack. Hit a fly ball to right.

It drifted… and drifted…

And then—holy shit.

A walk-off home run.

Shea exploded. Over 55,000 fans screaming, jumping, losing their minds. We stormed the field. I was ecstatic. I snuck a look into the stands—fans hugging, high-fiving, crying. It was a moment I'll never forget.

Some of the guys lifted Lenny like he was Rudy. It looked like a rock concert. Dykstra pumped his fist, tobacco juice glistening at the corner of his mouth.

One of the Mets staffers flashed a universal Italian "fuck you" toward the Astros dugout. No idea who it was for. It didn't matter.

At the press conference, Dykstra was classic.

"Y'all better not get used to this," he said.

The room lost it.

He was the man of the hour. And I was happy for him. He deserved that moment in the sun.

Sonny nodded. "That wasn't just a walk-off. That was a wake-up call. October had finally arrived."

Act 76: After the Game

"So, what did you do after the game?" Sonny asked.

I leaned back, still buzzing from the long afternoon. "After the game, I met up with Rafael and Junior."

We linked up at a little spot in Queens, the kind of place where the coffee's strong, the lights are dim, and the jukebox only plays old soul and salsa. We slid into a booth, still riding the high.

"That was one of the most impressive postseason games I've ever witnessed," Rafael said, shaking his head like he still couldn't believe it.

"Dykstra's a beast," Junior added, wide-eyed.

"I'm just happy we won," I said, sipping my coffee. "Two more to go. But tomorrow…we're facing fucking Mike Scott. That splitter is insane."

Junior grinned. "Yo, Jervin, remember when we were kids? We used to pretend you were on Kiner's Korner?"

I laughed. "Yeah. Let's do the bit for Rafael."

Junior slipped into his best Ralph Kiner voice, nasal and slow: "So, Jervin, you really hit the shit outta the ball tonight."

I dropped into my old-school hood rat voice: "Where's my shitty hundred-dollar bill, yo? Don't let me get ghetto up in this bitch."

Junior, still in character, leaned in: "You're going, going…and this motherfucker is outta here!"

We cracked up, loud and unfiltered. Heads turned. We didn't care.

It was our old routine. We used to do it all the time back when we were just kids with big dreams and busted gloves. We'd always end it the same way:

"Imagine if Ralph's goons came into the studio," I said, grinning, "took me out like Sonny Corleone, spit on the ground, and threw a couple hundred-dollar bills at my feet."

More laughter. The kind that makes your ribs hurt. The kind that reminds you who you are.

But it wasn't just the jokes. It was the remembrances. We remembered who we were growing up—kids with dreams.

Now? We were men with moments.

Sonny smiled, his eyes soft. "That's the kind of night you bottle. Not just for the win, but for the people who were there to laugh with you."

Act 77: The War Before the Battle

"Tell us about Game Four," Sonny said.

I took a breath, the memory still vivid. "Game Four was hours away. We were in the clubhouse, watching Boston face the California Angels in Game Five of the ALCS. The Angels were up three games to one, just three outs away from their first pennant."

The room was buzzing, but not with our own nerves—not yet. All eyes were on the screen.

"Both teams were stacked," I said. "I was staring at Doug DeCinces' high-five jump celebration. Quietly, I wanted the Angels to win. Not for them, but for us. I wanted to beat Reggie Jackson—the man who broke my heart when I was eleven."

I smiled at the memory. "That was the kid in me talking. My twenty-four-year-old self? He was buried in Houston's scouting report, trying to figure out how the hell we were gonna hit Mike Scott's splitter."

Still, the clubhouse was electric. The city was alive. Everyone was still talking about Dykstra's walk-off. Junior and Rafael said it was the most energy they'd felt since the 1981 Yankees. Sports are like what Janet Jackson once sang: *What have you done for me lately?*

So, we watched.

Bottom of the ninth. Angels up 5-2. Billy Buckner singled. Pinch runner Dave Stapleton came in. Jim Rice struck out. One out. Two to go.

Don Baylor worked a full count. Mike Witt threw a slider. Baylor crushed it to the left field seats. 5-4.

Still, the Angels had control.

Dwight Evans popped up. Two outs.

Rich Gedman stepped in. He'd already homered off Witt earlier, so Gene Mauch pulled Witt and brought in Gary Lucas, a lefty.

First pitch—Lucas hit Gedman.

Now the tying run was on.

Mauch made the slow walk again. Brought in Donnie Moore—Hubie Brooks' cousin. The room got quieter. More guys gathered around the TV.

Dave Henderson was Boston's last hope.

Moore had two strikes. His stuff was electric. Henderson kept fouling off pitch after pitch.

Then—crack.

Fly ball to left. It cleared the fence. 6-5, Boston.

The room let out a collective gasp. Some 'oohs' and 'ahhs.' We sat there, stunned. Not because we didn't care, but because we did.

That game reminded us: October doesn't forgive. It just moves forward.

Funny thing? Henderson had botched a play earlier in center. Gave up a homer. He was the goat. Now? He was the hero.

Bottom of the ninth. Boston three outs from forcing Game Six.

Bob Boone singled. Ruppert Jones pinch-ran. Gary Pettis bunted him to second.

Bob Stanley started the inning, but McNamara pulled him for Joe Sambito—Brooklyn born.

Rob Wilfong singled to right. Jones scored. Tie game, 6-6.

Sambito out. Steve Crawford in. Last-minute roster replacement for the injured…Tom Seaver. Yeah. That Tom Seaver.

Dick Schoefield singled. First and third. Winning run ninety feet away.

Doug DeCinces had his shot. Popped out to shallow right.

Then Bobby Grich stepped in. Weak liner. Inning over.

Extra Innings.

By now, the younger guys in the podcast were silent. Listening to me like I was telling a war story. Like I was some old vet telling them how it used to be.

Bottom of the tenth. Gary Pettis hit a deep fly. Jim Rice tracked it back to the wall and caught it against the fence.

Eleventh inning. Donnie Moore still pitching.

Don Baylor—hit by pitch. Classic Baylor.

Dwight Evans singled. Two on, no outs.

Gedman bunted. Misplayed. Bases loaded.

Dave Henderson again.

No place to put him.

Moore had to pitch to him.

Henderson hit a sac fly. Baylor scored. 7-6, Boston.

Bottom of the eleventh. Calvin Schiraldi came in. Yeah, that Schiraldi—from the Bobby Ojeda trade. He'd blown Game Four, but McNamara stuck with him.

This time, Schiraldi delivered. Shut the door.

Boston survived. Series now 3-2. Headed back to Fenway.

We sat there, drained. Like we'd played the game ourselves.

That's October baseball. It doesn't care about your feelings. It just moves.

Mike Scott was waiting for us. And we knew we'd need more than hope to beat him.

Rafael leaned over and said, "Watch how they win. That's how you learn to fight."

That afternoon, I was schooled.

Sonny nodded. "You watched a war. Now it was time to fight your own."

Act 78: Game Four and Five

"Okay," Sonny said. "Tell us about Game Four."

I shrugged. "Honestly, there's not much to say."

Mike Scott was in total control. A complete game. One run allowed. He dominated the mound from start to finish, like a conductor with a baton. Every pitch had purpose. Every inning, precision.

Sid Fernandez started for us. He gave up a homer to Dickie Thon. And that was it. Houston tied the series.

Sometimes, there's no drama. Just silence. Just a man with a splitter that danced like it had a soul.

We packed up, shook it off, and turned the page.

"Okay," Sonny said. "Tell us about Game Five."

I smiled. "Now that was a game."

Nolan Ryan vs. Dwight Gooden. Two flamethrowers. Two eras colliding.

The Astros struck first in the top of the fifth. But in the bottom half, Darryl Strawberry stepped in and launched one off Ryan. Tied it up, 1-1.

From there, it was a war of attrition. Pitch by pitch. Inning by inning. The game stretched into extras.

Bottom of the twelfth. Charlie Kerfeld was still on the mound—he'd taken over in the tenth.

Lenny Dykstra led off and grounded out. One away.

Wally Backman stepped in. He lined a shot that ricocheted off Denny Walling and bounced to short. Backman beat it out.

Then came Keith Hernandez. Kerfeld tried a pickoff move—threw it away. Backman advanced to second.

Houston intentionally walked Keith. Smart move. Gary Carter was hitting under .100 for the series. He'd been pressing. You could see it in his eyes.

But Carter worked the count to 3-1. Fouled one off. Then another. And another.

I glanced at Davey Johnson. The man looked like he needed a Rolaids and a prayer.

Then—Carter connected. A clean single up the middle.

I didn't just see the ball go through the infield—I saw a weight lift off his shoulders. Off all our shoulders.

Backman rounded third. Billy Hatcher's throw came in. Not on time.

Backman scored.

Walk-off win.

It was surreal. Like everything moved in slow motion. The crowd erupted. We mobbed Carter. The dugout emptied. It was chaos and clarity all at once.

We were up 3-2. One win away from the World Series.

The thought of it made my chest tighten in the best way.

After the game, I met up with Junior and Rafael.

"Dude," Junior said, doing his best Dykstra impression, "You guys are writing a movie script."

I laughed. "Feels like I'm living in a movie. I can't even describe it."

Rafael smiled. "Well, I'm glad we're riding this wave together. Good luck in Houston. I know you've got to pack."

I hugged them both. Held on a little longer than usual.

And I thought about Rafael's mantra: *Watch how they win. That's how you learn to fight.*

I was learning. Every game. Every pitch.

Sonny nodded. "One win away. And the script wasn't finished yet."

Act 79: Astrodome- Game Six

"So, you're in Houston and it's Game Six," Sonny said. "Tell us how that was."

I nodded, the memory still sharp.

"While we were flying to Houston, Boston blew out the Angels in Game Six. By the time we landed, the air was already heavy with October. You could feel it in your chest. It was like the whole city was holding its breath."

Bob Knepper was on the mound for them. Tough lefty. Crafty. He was dealing—had a two-hitter going into the ninth. We were down 3-0. The crowd was loud, but not wild. More like…expectant. They could smell blood.

Then came Lenny Dykstra.

Two quick strikes. Then he lifted a fly ball into the right-center gap. It dropped. Dykstra turned on the jets and stretched it into a leadoff triple.

Man on third. No outs.

Mookie Wilson stepped in. Knepper got ahead again—two strikes. But Mookie fought one off, fisted a line drive just over Bill Doran's glove. Dykstra scored.

Finally, we were on the board. 3-1.

Kevin Mitchell followed. Chopped a grounder to third. Out at first, but Mookie moved to second.

Then Keith Hernandez came up.

He ripped a double into the same right-center alley where Dykstra had tripled. Mookie scored. 3-2.

Now it was getting loud. But not from the crowd— from our dugout.

Knepper was done. Houston brought in Dave Smith, their closer. He was trying to shut the door. Trying to force a Game Seven.

Gary Carter stepped in. Worked the count full. Fouled off a couple. Then he drew a walk.

Two on, one out.

Darryl Strawberry followed. Another full count. Another walk.

Bases loaded.

Ray Knight stepped in.

He lifted a fly ball to deep right-center. Not a homer, but deep enough. Hernandez tagged and scored. Carter and Strawberry advanced.

The game was tied. 3-3.

The dugout erupted. We weren't just alive—we were awake. The Astrodome felt different. Like it knew something had shifted.

Wally Backman was next. Houston intentionally walked him.

Danny Heep came in to pinch-hit for Rick Aguilera. Bases loaded. Two outs.

Heep struck out.

We headed to the bottom of the ninth. Still tied.

Davey Johnson called on Roger McDowell.

Roger came in and set the Astros down in order. Calm. Cold. Clinical.

We exhaled.

Extra innings were coming.

And so was history.

Sonny nodded, his voice low. "You tied the game, but you hadn't tied the story. That was still waiting."

Act 80: The Marathon

"You call this 'The Marathon'," Sonny said.

I nodded. "It was a marathon."

The score was tied at three. Extra innings loomed. The Astrodome felt like a pressure cooker—thick air, tight chests, every pitch a coin flip.

Neither team scored in the tenth. Or the eleventh. Or the twelfth.

By the thirteenth, the game had taken on a mythic quality. Later, I'd learn that back in New York, crowds were gathering outside storefronts, watching the broadcast through glowing windows. Rafael and Junior had set up a TV in our shop window. A crowd pressed in, shoulder to shoulder, riding every pitch with us.

Top of the fourteenth. Aurelio Lopez took the mound—built like he hadn't missed a meal in years.

Gary Carter led off with a single. Strawberry followed with a walk. The dugout stirred. You could feel it—something was coming.

Ray Knight tried to bunt them over. Lopez pounced, fired to third. Carter was out.

One away.

Then Wally Backman stepped in. He lined a single to right. Strawberry scored. The dugout erupted—bats banging, voices screaming, frustration spilling out as joy.

Kevin Bass's throw home was wild. Knight and Backman advanced.

The pennant was within reach.

But Houston wasn't done.

Bottom of the fourteenth. Jesse Orosco came in to close. Two outs. Billy Hatcher at the plate.

Full count.

Orosco fired a fastball.

Crack.

Hatcher launched it down the left field line.

Fair. Gone.

Tie game.

The Astrodome exploded. My stomach dropped. If we lost, Mike Scott was waiting for Game Seven. And none of us wanted that fate.

Fifteenth inning. Carter singled again but was thrown out trying to advance on a wild pitch. Orosco held the Astros down at the bottom of the inning.

Then came the sixteenth.

History.

The longest postseason game ever at the time.

By then, I wasn't thinking about champagne. I was thinking about coffee.

Strawberry blooped a ball into the gap—bounced high off the turf for a double.

Knight followed with a single to right. Strawberry scored.

Textbook hitting. Contact. Bat control. Going the other way. George's lessons from my childhood echoed in my head.

Lopez was pulled. Jeff Calhoun entered.

Chaos followed.

Wild pitch—Knight to third.

Backman walked.

Another wild pitch—Knight scored.

6-4.

The dugout shook with belief.

Orosco bunted Backman to third.

Dykstra singled him home.

7-4.

The Astrodome crowd began to thin. They could feel it slipping away.

But October never lets go easy.

Orosco struck out Craig Reynolds to start the bottom of the sixteenth. Two outs away.

Then Davey Lopes walked.

Bill Doran singled.

Billy Hatcher—already a hero once—singled again. 7-5.

The tying run was on base.

My heart was pounding. I could feel it in my throat. I was shaking my head, muttering under my breath, begging for Rolaids.

Denny Walling stepped in. He chopped one to Hernandez at first. Keith scooped it clean, fired to second— force play.

Two down.

One to go.

Then Glenn Davis blooped a single into shallow right. Just out of the reach of Backman and Strawberry.

7-6.

The winning run was now on base.

The Astrodome came alive again. The place had lungs. It roared like it knew we were on the ropes.

I looked at Orosco. He was pacing the mound, breathing heavily, but his eyes were locked in. No fear. Just fire.

Kevin Bass stepped in.

The count ran full.

Three balls. Two strikes. Two outs. Bottom of the sixteenth. Two men on. One-run lead. The season in danger.

I could barely breathe.

Orosco nodded to Carter. Set. Delivered.

Slider.

Bass swung.

Missed.

Strike three.

Game over.

We exploded.

Harry Albino

Orosco flung his glove into the air like a man launching a flare into the night. Carter leapt into his arms. The dugout emptied. We stormed the field like kids on the last day of school.

We had done it.

We survived the marathon.

We were going to the World Series.

My childhood fantasy had become a reality.

Later that night, Boston clinched their own pennant.

The matchups were set.

Act 81: Mets versus Red Sox

The ghosts of 1986 stirred.

Our next mission awaited.

The city didn't sleep. Not really, for Mets fans. Radios buzzed in bodegas. Taxi drivers leaned out of windows, shouting predictions. Strangers high-fived on subway platforms. It was like the whole city had been holding its breath for thirteen years, and now it was ready to exhale—one inning at a time.

For me, it was different.

I didn't go out. Didn't celebrate.

I sat in my hotel room, lights off, TV on mute, watching the highlights of our game on loop. Sixteen innings. One dream. And now, a new mountain to climb.

Act 82: Homecoming

The flight back to New York felt like a dream.

I didn't expect the crowd at LaGuardia.

The place was packed. Fans pressed against barricades, waving signs, chanting "Let's Go Mets!" like it was a Broadway chorus. Children sat on their fathers' shoulders. Old-timers wore faded 1969 jerseys. One guy blasted *Eye of the Tiger* from a boombox balanced on his shoulder like it was still 1982.

I wasn't a star—not like Strawberry, Carter, Hernandez, or Gooden.

But that day, I felt like one.

A police officer gave me a fist pump. A woman slipped a bracelet of orange and blue beads into my hand. Someone shouted, "Jervin, you're the soul of the team!"

I laughed. But the words stuck.

We weren't just heading to the World Series.

We were carrying the hopes of a city that hadn't danced in October in a long, long time.

The ride back to Manhattan was surreal. The skyline shimmered like a promise.

Rafael and Junior were waiting at the condo. Rafael had a bottle of champagne chilling—not for celebration, but for symbolism.

"We're not popping this until you win it all," he said.

Junior was already sketching ideas for Jura-Class gear with a World Series theme. He had the look in his eye— the one he got when inspiration hit like lightning.

I thought about my parents in Bellmore, watching the news and smiling. I thought about RJ asleep in Queens, unaware his uncle was about to play on the biggest stage in baseball.

I didn't sleep much that night.

My mind kept replaying the final out in Houston— Carter's knees buckling, Orosco's fist in the air, the pile of bodies on the mound.

The World Series was next.

Boston was waiting,

And so was destiny.

Act 83: The World Series - Game One

"Now you're living the dream," Sonny said. "Tell us about your first experience in the World Series."

I smiled. "The Series couldn't have been more ideal."

Vin Scully's voice carried through the stadium like scripture. Every pitch, every pause, every breath he made it feel sacred.

Before the first pitch, I glanced toward the Boston dugout.

And there he was.

Tom Seaver.

The man who had defined Mets baseball. Now wearing a Red Sox uniform.

It didn't seem right. But that was the nature of the business. Heroes don't always stay home.

Ron Darling was our starter. Bruce Hurst, Boston's tough lefty, stood opposite him. From the first inning, it was a duel.

Bill Buckner came up early, wearing high-top cleats, unusually, but necessary for his bad ankles. He grounded into a double play. I was part of turning it.

For me, that was more thrilling than most realized.

The game settled into rhythm. Darling matched Hurst pitch for pitch. Somewhere in the stands, I knew Junior and Rafael were watching, urging me to log every detail of this run.

And thank God I did.

Top of the seventh. Darling walked Jim Rice. Dwight Evans stepped in. A wild pitch sent Rice to second. Evans hit a comebacker. Darling held Rice, threw Evans out. Smooth. He was a Gold Glove fielder, and it showed.

Then Rich Gedman hit a grounder at Tim Teufel.

It skipped under his glove. Rolled into right field.

Rice raced home.

Strawberry's throw came in hot. Darling collided with the on-deck hitter, Dave Henderson, behind the plate. A freak accident. No one was hurt.

Boston led, 1-0.

Top of the ninth. Two on. Henderson singled.

Evans tried to score.

Kevin Mitchell fired a strike from left. Carter tagged him out at the plate.

Fifty-five thousand fans finally had something to cheer for.

Boston loaded the bases after an intentional walk to Spike Owen. Hurst was due up, but McNamara sent Mike Greenwell to pinch-hit.

Roger McDowell delivered.

Greenwell flied out to Dykstra.

Threat ended.

Bottom of the ninth.

Calvin Schiraldi came into close.

We met him. He'd been one of us once, back in the minors. Quiet guy. Good arm. Now he was wearing Boston red, trying to slam the door on his old organization.

Strawberry led off.

Worked out a walk.

The crowd rose—fifty-five thousand strong— screaming, pleading for ninth-inning magic.

Ray Knight squared to bunt. Laid it down.

Dave Stapleton—Buckner's late-inning defense replacement—charged, fielded, and fired to second.

Out.

Strawberry erased.

One down.

Wally Backman stepped in. Took a hack. Lifted a fly ball to shallow left.

Caught.

Two outs.

Then came Danny Heep.

Pinch-hitting for me. Again.

I wanted that moment. I wanted it bad. But baseball is a team sport. You check your ego at the dugout steps.

Heep dug in.

Swung through strike three.

Game over.

Just like that, we were down 1-0 in the Series.

The crowd deflated. The scoreboard glared. The walk back to the clubhouse felt longer than usual.

Sonny leaned in. "Game One slipped away. But the dream wasn't over—it was only beginning."

I nodded. "Exactly. October doesn't hand you anything. You've got to take it."

Act 84: Game Two - The Chain

"Okay," Sonny said. "You're down 1-0 and entering Game Two. What are your thoughts—and what happened?"

I leaned back, the memory still sharp.

"Game Two was supposed to be a marquee matchup. Dwight Gooden versus Roger Clemens. Two young fireballers. Two aces. Two cities with everything on the line."

Davey Johnson shook up the lineup. He started Danny Heep in left field. Most of the year, Heep had been a reserve outfielder, a pinch hitter. But Davey Johnson had a knack for these kinds of moves. He was one of the first managers to use a computer for game analysis. There's a story—don't know if it's true—that he once handed Earl Weaver a printout of stats and matchups, and Weaver just tossed it in the trash. That was Davey, though. Part gut, part algorithm.

He also started Howard Johnson at third. Ray Knight had been our guy all postseason, but Davey saw something. He always did.

Before the game, I spotted Rafael and Junior near the tunnel.

"Guys," I said, "I've got a surprise for you."

They looked at me, curious.

"I purchased you tickets to Games Three and Four in Boston. Plane tickets. Hotel. Everything. It's all set."

They froze.

"Dude," Junior said, pulling me into a hug. "Thank you."

Junior smiled, eyes glassy. Rafael didn't say a word. He just took off his gold chain—the one with the cross—and placed it around my neck.

It felt like receiving the Presidential Medal of Honor.

"What's this for?" I asked.

"For good luck," he said. "No matter what happens, wear it for the entire series."

I nodded. I felt honored. Like I was carrying something sacred.

Before the game, Elie Wiesel threw out the first pitch. The winner of the 1986 Nobel Peace Prize. Author. Activist. Holocaust survivor. An interesting man with an even more interesting life. His presence reminded us that baseball, for all its drama, was still just a game.

The first two innings were a pitcher's duel. Gooden and Clemens were dealing fastballs like lightning, breaking balls like whispers.

Then came the top of the third.

Spike Owen led off with a walk. Clemens came up to bunt. He laid it down, and Keith Hernandez charged. Made a throw to second—but it was off. I couldn't field the throw. Un-Hernandez-like. Suddenly, first and second. No outs.

Wade Boggs stepped in. Doubled down the left-field line. Owens scored. Clemens held at third. Boggs on second.

1-0, Boston.

Marty Barrett singled to right-center. Clemens scored. Boggs held at third.

2-0.

Then Buckner singled to right. Boggs scored. Barrett to second.

3-0.

Things weren't looking good.

But Gooden dug deep. Struck out Dwight Evans. Then Rich Gedman. He stopped the bleeding.

Still, I had to admit—Boston didn't look like underdogs. They played like the favorites. Tough. Focused. Unshaken.

Bottom of the third. I led off.

And it happened.

I singled off the Rocket Man.

I was so thrilled, I asked for the ball. And unbelievably, they gave it to me.

My first World Series hit.

To the casual fan, it's just a single.

To me? It was everything.

Gooden came up next. He tried to bunt. Popped it up. Buckner couldn't manage it.

Two on. No outs.

Fifty-five thousand fans came alive.

Lenny Dykstra stepped in.

"Come on, dude," I whispered.

He laid down a perfect bunt. Moved us both up.

Backman followed. Singled. I came home.

Touching that plate—it was like reaching Mecca.

Gooden moved to third. One out.

Keith Hernandez hit a one-hopper off Clemens' foot. Boggs made a great play. Got him at first. But Gooden scored.

3-2.

Boggs was everywhere. The scouting report said he was a mediocre fielder. What it didn't tell you was how big a man's heart could be.

Top of the fourth. Dave Henderson led off.

He went yard.

4-2, Boston.

Bottom of the fourth. I did it again. Another single. I was feeling it. Seeing the ball like it was a beach ball.

Top of the fifth. Jim Rice singled. Then Dwight Evans crushed a two-run homer.

6-2.

And honestly? After that, I knew it was over.

Boston went on to rout us, 9-3.

We were down 2-0 in the Series.

After the game, I met with Rafael and Junior.

"Boy, you guys got your asses kicked tonight," Junior said, grinning.

"Gooden's fastball was flat," Rafael added.

I laughed. "Honestly? It was your chain."

Rafael cracked up.

"I'll meet you guys in Boston," I said.

I hugged them both.

Then I turned around, still in uniform, and headed toward the tunnel.

Fenway was waiting.

Act 85: Game 3 - The Green Monster and The Dead Fish

"So, it's Game Three of the World Series," Sonny said. "This was your first trip to Fenway Park. What was it like?"

I smiled. "Looking at the thirty-seven-foot Big Green Monster was like staring at a piece of not just baseball history—but American history. It was built the same year the Titanic sank. You feel that when you're standing there. Like the ghosts of the game are watching."

I'd never been to Boston before. Junior had—he's got family there, and he knew the landscape. Me? I was just soaking it all in.

The starters for Game Three were Dennis "Oil Can" Boyd for Boston and Bobby Ojeda for us. The scouting report said Boyd was 'high-strung.' There was more to it than that.

Before the game, Tip O'Neill—the retiring Speaker of the House, and a proud Bostonian—threw out the first pitch. The crowd roared. It felt like a political rally and a church revival all at once.

Then came Lenny Dykstra.

Leadoff hitter. Spark plug. Maniac.

First pitch—boom.

Fly ball to right. It carried. Landed in the stands.

1-0, Mets.

Just like that, the pressure cracked. It was the first time we'd led in the Series.

Backman followed with a single to right. Then Keith Hernandez laced one into left-center. Backman hustled to third.

John McNamara made an early trip to the mound. Oil Can was already slinging bullets.

With two on and no outs, Gary Carter stepped in and ripped a gapper to left-center. Backman scored. Hernandez pulled up at third.

2-0.

Strawberry struck out—his seventeenth K of the postseason. He was pressing. You could see it in his swing.

Ray Knight hit a grounder at Boggs. Boggs threw home. Gedman chased Hernandez back to third, then flipped to Spike Owen, who tried to run Carter back to second. Everyone ended up safe.

Bases loaded.

Then came Danny Heep, our first-ever designated hitter in a World Series game. Johnson had inserted him into the lineup, and it paid off.

Heep singled to center. Hernandez scored. Carter scored.

4-0.

The dugout erupted. Bats clanged. Fists pumped. We were alive.

Mookie struck out. I ended the inning with a grounder to Boggs. But the tone was set.

Bobby Ojeda took the mound in the bottom of the first.

He'd been traded from Boston in the offseason. Now he was facing his old team on the biggest stage in baseball. He was the first pitcher in World Series history to start a game against the team that traded him the year before.

Ojeda had a changeup he called "the dead fish."

We needed that fish to swim tonight.

He cruised through the first two innings. But in the bottom of the third, Dave Henderson singled. One out later, Boggs singled to left. Then Marty Barrett punched one between a diving Hernandez and Backman. Henderson scored.

4-1.

First and second. One out. The crowd started to buzz. Fenway was waking up.

Ojeda struck out Buckner. Then Jim Rice hit a hard grounder at me. I flipped it to Backman. Threat ended.

Bottom of the fifth. Two outs. Boggs singled. Barrett followed with a single to center.

Bob Murphy's voice echoed in my head: "This is the moment of truth."

Buckner hit a slow roller at me. I fielded it clean, flipped to Backman. Inning over.

Ojeda was pitching like a magician.

Top of the seventh. One out. I singled up the middle—my third hit of the series.

Dykstra followed with a single to right. Backman popped up. Hernandez walked.

Bases loaded.

McNamara made another slow walk to the mound. Took Oil Can's temperature.

Left him in.

Carter stepped in. Singled.

I scored. Dykstra scored.

6-1.

That took the air out of Boston's sails.

Bottom of the seventh. Henderson walked. The Boston crowd started the wave. I'll admit—I liked the wave. Just not against us.

Spike Owen hit a grounder to second. Backman flipped it to me. I danced across the bag and fired to Hernandez.

Double play.

Rafael's voice echoed in my head from the dugout: "Dance with the dirt, kid."

Ojeda ended the inning. Still 6-1.

Top of the eighth. Boston brought in Joe Sambito— fellow New Yorker.

Strawberry greeted him with a single. I felt relief for Darryl. He'd been pressing hard.

Sambito threw a wild pitch. Then, Gedman let one get past him.

Strawberry to third.

Ray Knight doubled down the third-base line.

7-1.

That took the wind out of Boston's sails.

Bottom of the eighth. Davey brought in Roger McDowell. He shut them down.

Top of the ninth. Dykstra reached on an infield hit—his fourth of the game. First Met to ever do that in a World Series.

Bottom of the ninth. McDowell closed it out. Impeccable.

We won Game Three.

Still down 2-1 in the Series.

But the tide had shifted.

Later that night, I met up with Rafael and Junior for a bite.

"Dykstra is a beast," Junior said, shaking his head.

"Tonight, bro," Rafael added, "you danced with the dirt. That was a sweet-ass double play you turned."

That made my night.

I needed rest.

The Big Green Monster was waiting.

Act 86: Game 4 - Going Yard

"So, it's Game Four," Sonny said. "A crucial game. Tell us about it."

"The starting pitchers were Al Nipper and Ron Darling," I said. "Darling was making his second start of the Series. Nipper, his first. Both managers stuck with the same lineups from Game Three."

In the bottom of the first, Boston came out swinging. Marty Barrett doubled. Jim Rice and Don Baylor walked. Bases loaded. One out.

Dwight Evans hit a grounder at me. I scooped it, flipped it to Backman. Inning over. Crisis averted.

Top of the fourth: Backman singled. On a hit-and-run, Boston called a pitchout. Hernandez somehow made contact—pure instinct—and moved Backman to second.

Then Gary Carter stepped in. And launched one. Over the Green Monster.

I jumped up like a little kid. Couldn't help it.

2-0, Mets.

Strawberry followed with a double down the left field line. Ray Knight lined a single to center. Strawberry scored. 3-0.

Darling kept dodging bullets. In the bottom of the fifth, Boston had runners on first and third with two outs. Darling worked his magic. Another bullet dodged.

Still 3-0.

Bottom of the sixth: Carter was cut down on the plate in the top half. Then Rich Gedman ripped a liner to the left field corner. Evans went to third. Gedman tried to stretch it into a double. Bad idea. He was gunned down.

Top of the seventh: Steve Crawford replaced Nipper. Mookie Wilson singled with one out. With two outs, he stole second and advanced to third on a throwing error by Rich Gedman.

Then Dykstra stepped in. Hit a fly ball to right.

Evans tracked it. Reached over the fence. The ball hit the tip of his glove.

Home run.

Dykstra—the smallest guy on the team—had homered for the second night in a row.

Evans stood there, arms draped over the fence, frozen.

5-0.

The game was slipping away from Boston.

Fenway was quiet. Like a wake in a funeral home. I heard a few cheers—probably Junior and Rafael, screaming and whistling from the stands.

Bottom of the seventh: Darling walked Spike Owen and Marty Barrett. Two outs. Buckner popped one up—right to me.

Inning over.

Darling was dancing between the raindrops. Not dominant, but damn effective.

Top of the eighth: One out. Carter stepped in again.

Rocket launcher.

Cleared the Green Monster. Cleared the park.

6-0.

We were inching closer to tying the Series.

Inside, I was buzzing. But on the field, I stayed stoic. A win tonight meant a guaranteed trip back to New York. At least one more game in front of the Shea faithful.

Bottom of the eighth: Davey Johnson brought in Roger McDowell. Darling's night was done.

Rice led off with a double. Baylor hit a line drive—I snagged it. Evans singled. Rice scored.

6-1.

Gedman singled. First and third. One out.

Dave Henderson hit a fly to right. Deep enough. Evans scored.

6-2.

Boston was stirring.

My philosophy? If you're down four or fewer, you're one big swing away from tying the game.

Spike Owen was due up. McNamara sent up Mike Greenwell.

McDowell walked him.

Didn't have it tonight.

Davey went to the pen. Called for Jesse Orosco.

Two outs. Two on. Wade Boggs at the plate.

Boggs bounced one to me.

I was positioned perfectly.

Fielded it. Flipped to Backman.

Threat ended.

Orosco shut them down in the ninth.

Just like that, the World Series was tied.

After the game, I met up with Rafael and Junior at the Eliot Lounge. Junior knew the spot—said it was a stylish hangout for athletes, writers, and locals.

I'd been on TV, sure. But I wasn't a famous face like Keith Hernandez. I just wanted to blend in. Listen to the chatter.

"Dykstra is a fucking beast," Junior said, shaking his head.

"Darling was dancing with danger all night," Rafael added. "Pulled a Houdini."

"I gotta admit," I said, grinning. "Those Carter homers? Rocket launchers."

Rafael leaned in. "How about tomorrow?"

"Bruce Hurst," I said. "He's tough. Not Mike Scott tough. But close."

We didn't stay long. Just a quick bite. A few laughs.

Game Five was less than twenty-four hours away.

And now?

Now the stakes were higher.

We were back in the game.

Act 87: Game 5—Bruce Gem vs. Darryl Touts

"So now the Mets are tied with Boston, 2-2," Sonny said. "A crucial Game Five is at stake. Tell us about it."

"It was a heavyweight matchup," I said. "Bruce Hurst, Boston's tough lefty, against our ace, Dwight Gooden. Doc had been flat in Game Two—we were hoping that was just an aberration."

Fenway was electric. The crowd was deafening, especially when Ted Williams came out to throw the ceremonial first pitch. We're talking about an icon. A war hero. A Hall of Famer. The place shook.

Bottom of the first. Marty Barrett walked with one out. Then, out of nowhere, Gooden picked him off. That surprised me—Doc wasn't known for pickoffs. Darling was the head of that. But Doc got him.

Two outs. Buckner singled up the middle. Then Jim Rice hit a grounder that ricocheted off the mound. Teufel couldn't manage it—it clipped his ankle. They ruled it a hit. Generous, if you ask me.

Then Gooden plunked Don Baylor. Bases loaded.

But Doc got Evans to fly out to left. Threat ended. Another bullet dodged.

Bottom of the second. Dave Henderson tripled to right-center. Dykstra slipped on the warning track from the rain earlier. That slip might've been the difference.

Spike Owen hit a fly ball to left. Henderson tagged and scored easily. Boston led, 1-0.

Top of the third. I led off with a walk. I swear I could hear Junior and Rafael whistling from the stands. Hurst kept throwing over to first. I had zero intention of stealing. None.

Dykstra dumped a single into center. Two on, no outs.

Teufel came up. Off the bat, it sounded like he got all of it. I thought it was going to hit the Green Monster. Instead, just a loud out.

Bottom of the third. Buckner hit a grounder at me.

And I booted it.

It was my first error in eleven postseason games.

I could already picture Rafael's face—he always made this look like someone had just farted in the room whenever I made an error.

Rice walked. Baylor struck out. Then Evans singled to center. Buckner, bad wheels and all, scored from second.

2-0, Boston.

Gedman flied out to end the inning.

Top of the fifth. Kevin Mitchell led off with a single. Mookie followed with a single to left. I was sent up to bunt.

I laid it down the third base line. Hurst couldn't get to it, but Boggs did. Gunned me at first. Almost beat it out. But I did my job—moved the runners.

Second and third. One out.

Dykstra struck out, Teufel grounded out.

Hurst shut us down again.

Bottom of the fifth. Rice led off with a triple—just missed a homer by a few feet. Then Baylor blooped a single to right. Rice scored.

3-0.

Momentum was shifting. You could feel it.

Evans hit a grounder in the hole for a single. Davey had seen enough. He pulled Gooden and brought in Sid Fernandez—El Sid.

Fernandez struck out Gedman on three pitches. His fastball looked electric.

But Henderson ripped a double past Ray Knight in the left-field corner. Baylor scored.

4-0.

Spike Owen hit a hard grounder. Teufel made a nice play to end the inning.

That fifth inning lasted half an hour. My knees were cold. I should've worn long johns. Rookie mistake.

Top of the sixth. Hurst mowed us down in order. Boston was feeling it. You could see it in their eyes.

Top of the eighth. Teufel finally broke through as he hit a home run into the right-field stands.

4-1.

Hernandez singled to right. Carter grounded to second. Two outs.

The crowd was roaring. Thirty-three thousand sounded like a coliseum.

Strawberry popped out to third.

In the bottom of the eighth, the Boston fans started taunting Darryl.

"Darryl…Darrryl…Darryl…"

He took off his cap and acknowledged them. But they kept going.

I kept glancing toward right field. I couldn't imagine what was going through his mind. We were both just kids—twenty-four—playing on the biggest stage in the world.

Boggs hit a liner that Teufel couldn't manage. Nailed him in the ankle. That had to hurt.

Barrett doubled off the Monster. That hit set a postseason record at the time—most hits in the postseason, breaking Thurman Munson's mark.

Two outs. Buckner popped up to Ray Knight.

Off to the ninth.

McNamara let Hurst start the inning. I saw Calvin Schiraldi warming in the pen, just in case.

Dave Stapleton came in for Buckner at first.

Hurst got two quick outs.

Then Mookie doubled to left.

I was the last hope.

I've always hated making the last out. Even in Little League.

So, I delivered.

Opposite field single. Mookie scored.

My first career World Series RBI.

I didn't show it, but I was proud.

4-2.

Dykstra was the tying run.

McNamara stuck with the lefty-on-lefty matchup.

Hurst struck him out.

Game over.

Complete game for Bruce Hurst. In today's game, that's unthinkable. Back then? That was October baseball.

We had to fly out right after the game. No time to see Rafael or Junior. I'd have to wait until we got back to New York.

Our backs were against the wall.

Down 3-2 in the series.

And as the old cliché goes— There is no tomorrow.

Act 88: The Calm Before the Storm

"So, it's Friday," Sonny said. "The day before the biggest game of your career. What did you do to relax?"

"Well," I said, grinning, "unlike what people think, I wasn't curled up in a fetal position."

I laughed.

"I went to dinner with Rafael, Junior, and Juanita. We were enjoying our steak dinners—well done, all of us— when a fan approached our table. Middle-aged white guy, thick Brooklyn accent. Looked like he'd just stepped out of a Scorsese film."

"Yous gotta win tomorrow," he said. "I'm betting on the game."

We all looked at each other. No one said a word.

Finally, I broke the silence. "Can I help you with something, sir?"

The man reached into his coat.

Junior stood up and grabbed him by his wrist.

"What do you have in your coat?" he asked.

"It's not like that," the man said quickly. "I just want an autograph."

Junior looked at me. I shook my head.

"I was just reaching for a paper and pen," the man added.

The manager noticed the commotion and came over. "Is everything okay?"

Junior was still standing.

"Yes," I said. "This man just wanted an autograph before he left the restaurant."

That was my diplomatic way of getting rid of him.

After he left, Junior still looked tense.

"Relax," I said. "You don't want to go to jail for beating up a senior citizen."

Juanita laughed. "He wasn't that old."

I turned to Rafael. "This chain better work. Otherwise, I'm melting it down and making earrings."

We all cracked up.

Then we raised our glasses.

"To the World Series," I said. "May all our dreams come true."

Other than the interruption, it felt like home again. Like the night before a big test, but with people who believed in you.

Sonny leaned in. "There's one question I haven't asked you yet. Why did you wear number zero your entire career?"

I smiled. "There's a story behind that."

"When I was in seventh grade, we had something called Career Day. I was in public school at the time. One of the counselors—Mr. Pomerantz—asked me what I wanted to do after high school. What my goals were."

I said, "What makes you think finishing high school is my only goal?"

He blinked. "Oh? So, what are your plans?"

Mr. Pomerantz was this balding, middle-aged guy who looked like he'd rather be working in private school but had to settle for a city job.

"I plan on attending college," I told him. "I have no desire to work in some factory or settle for a mediocre job."

He nodded, then said, "Okay, but hypothetically, let's say you don't attend college. Are you interested in vocational school?"

He handed me some brochures.

I put them on the desk.

"I have no plans to attend vocational school. I have no plans to build a machine. I plan to be a cog."

He ignored that and kept talking about trade schools.

I cut him off. "Listen, my dream is to make it to the Major Leagues. My backup dream is to be a doctor, a lawyer, or serve in the military. Maybe law enforcement. My bar is higher than yours."

He went silent.

I wasn't trying to be disrespectful. I just didn't want to be boxed in. I'd seen what happened to men like my father—working themselves into the ground for a paycheck that barely paid the bills.

After a pause, he said, "I was merely suggesting—"

I cut him off again. "I know what you were suggesting. You think I'm going to be nothing. I'll tell you what—when I make the majors, I'm going to wear number zero. Because that's what you think of me. And every time you see me on TV, that zero will remind you to never underestimate a kid like me."

He thought I was full of shit. I left the brochures on the desk and walked out.

I picked them up and dumped them in the trash on my way out.

Sonny shook his head. "Wow. That took a lot of balls. You must've been, what—thirteen?"

"Yeah," I said. "But I knew what I wanted. And I knew I had to be twice as good as my counterparts. They were allowed to be average. I had to be extraordinary."

Act 89: Game 6—Miracle Mets 2.0

"It was a Saturday night," I told Sonny. "New York was buzzing. The whole nation was watching. And if I said I wasn't nervous, I'd be lying."

Before the game, I gave Darryl Strawberry a fist bump. No words. Just that. He knew what it meant—I was with him. Have been since 1983.

All day Friday into Saturday afternoon, the sports talk shows were relentless. Every host, every caller, every so-called expert had the same take: if we lost Game 6, the season was a failure. We'd won 108 games—a franchise record. On paper, we were the best team in baseball.

But paper doesn't win championships.

The pitching matchup was a study in contrast. Bobby Ojeda and his "dead fish" changeup versus Roger Clemens, the Rocket Man, throwing pure heat.

From the very first pitch, Shea Stadium was electric.

Top of the first. Wade Boggs hit a liner at Ray Knight. It deflected off his glove and rolled toward me. I didn't have enough time to make a play. Boggs was safe with a single.

Then, with Buckner at the plate, the most New York thing happened.

The crowd started cheering louder than usual. I turned toward the outfield and saw a man parachuting onto the field, a giant "Go Mets" banner trailing behind him. He landed between the mound and first base, then calmly walked toward the police and gave himself up.

I couldn't help it—I was grinning ear to ear. It was hilarious. That was New York for you.

Back to the game. With two outs, Jim Rice walked. Then Dwight Evans doubled off the left-center field wall. Boggs scored.

Boston led, 1-0.

Top of the second. Spike Owen singled with one out. With two outs, he took off running. Boggs singled to right-center. Owen, flying around the bases, was held at third. I thought he'd score from first, but they played it safe.

Then Marty Barrett—our personal tormentor—singled to left. Owen scored.

2-0, Boston.

Clemens was dealing. Through four innings, we didn't have a hit.

Bottom of the fifth. Darryl led off with a walk. Then, with Ray Knight at the plate, he stole second. On a 2-2 count, Knight singled up the middle. Darryl came flying home.

2-1.

Mookie followed with a single to right. Evans misplayed the hop—it bounced off his chest. Knight hustled from first to third.

First and third. Nobody out.

Then Davey Johnson made a move.

He lifted me for a pinch hitter.

Danny Heep.

I was stunned. Disappointed. I had to sit and become a spectator.

Heep grounded into a double play. Knight scored. We tied the game, 2-2.

But I wasn't celebrating.

Dances with the Dirt

Top of the sixth. Kevin Elster came in at short.

I didn't say anything. Didn't show it. But it felt like a dagger to the chest.

I walked into the clubhouse. Alone. Sat down. Thought about everything it took to get here. The hours. The setbacks. The sacrifices.

But I had to get over it. Fast.

This was bigger than me. I wanted that ring. And yeah, the $80K bonus didn't hurt either.

I took a deep breath. Composed myself. And went back to the dugout.

Top of the seventh. Davey Johnson made the call to the bullpen and brought in Roger McDowell. Hard to believe McDowell had won fourteen games as a reliever that season. Fourteen. That's unheard of.

Marty Barrett led off with a walk. On a hit-and-run, Buckner grounded to second, moving Barrett into scoring position.

Then Jim Rice hit a chopper to Ray Knight. Knight fielded it cleanly—but rushed the throw. It sailed high. Rice reached on the error.

Now Boston had runners on the corners.

With a full count, and Rice running on the pitch, Dwight Evans grounded to Backman. Wally flipped it to Elster at second base. Rice beat the throw, but they got Evans at first.

Barrett scored.

Boston retook the lead, 3-2.

With Rice on second and two outs, Rich Gedman singled to left. Mookie charged the ball and came up firing.

He gunned out Rice at the plate.

That throw saved the inning—and the game.

Top of the eighth. Dave Henderson reached on an infield hit off Elster. Spike Owen laid down a sacrifice, moving Henderson to second.

Clemens was due up, but McNamara sent up Mike Greenwell to pinch-hit.

McDowell struck him out.

Wade Boggs was intentionally walked.

Then Marty Barrett—again—drew a walk.

Bases loaded.

Davey Johnson didn't wait. He brought in Jesse Orosco.

He didn't want to. Orosco was due to lead off the bottom of the eighth. But this was Game 6. All bets were off.

Orosco did his job.

Boston stranded three.

Bottom of the eighth. Six outs from elimination.

McNamara brought in his closer, Calvin Schiraldi, for a six-out save.

Lee Mazzilli pinch-hit for Orosco.

He singled to right.

The crowd came alive.

Lenny Dykstra tried to bunt. Schiraldi fielded it, but his throw to second was low. Mazzilli slid in safe.

Two on. No outs.

Backman laid down a perfect sacrifice. Both runners advanced.

One out. Second and third.

McNamara ordered an intentional walk to Keith Hernandez.

Bases loaded.

The fans were on their feet. I could feel the concrete shake beneath me. Shea was built on a meadow, and for a second, I thought it might sink.

Gary Carter stepped in.

Lifted a fly ball to left. Deep enough.

Mazzilli tagged and scored.

Tie game. 3-3.

The place exploded.

Strawberry flied out to end the inning, but the damage was done.

Davey made a double switch—left Mazzilli in to play right, pulled Strawberry, and brought in Rick Aguilera to pitch.

Aguilera held the line in the top of the ninth.

Now it was our turn.

Bottom of the ninth.

We had a chance to walk it off. To send this thing to Game 7. To shake Shea to its foundation.

We flipped our caps inside out.

Rally caps.

Ballplayers are superstitious by nature. This was our mythical way of asking the baseball gods for one more miracle.

Ray Knight led off.

Drew a walk.

Then Mookie Wilson laid down a bunt.

The throw to second was high.

Knight was safe. Owen's foot was off the bag.

The ump got it right.

McNamara stormed out of the dugout, arguing the call.

Now we had two on, no outs. The winning run on second.

Davey Johnson sent up Howard Johnson to pinch-hit for Elster.

Hojo was asked to bunt.

He failed.

Fouled-tipped a pitch right into Gedman's mitt. Strike three.

Mazzilli flied to left. Two outs.

It was up to Lenny Dykstra.

We were going to extras.

More drama added to Game 6.

Top of the tenth. Rick Aguilera still on the mound.

Dave Henderson led off.

Fly ball. Left field.

Gone.

4-3, Boston.

Shea went silent.

My stomach turned. Flashbacks hit my senior year of high school, the College World Series. That hollow, sinking feeling.

Losing sucks.

I looked at the Red Sox dugout. They had that look. That we're about to be champions look.

Two outs later, Wade Boggs doubled.

Then Marty Barrett—our worst nightmare—singled him home.

5-3, Boston.

Jim Rice flied out to Mazzilli. The bleeding stopped.

Some fans left.

Most stayed.

Bottom of the tenth. Wally Backman led off.

Weak fly to left. One out.

Keith Hernandez flied to Henderson.

Two outs.

One more to go.

Dances with the Dirt

I muttered under my breath, "108 fucking wins and this is how it ends."

Gary Carter stepped in.

Our last hope.

He singled to left.

We were still alive.

Kevin Mitchell was called to pinch-hit for Aguilera.

Problem was Mitchell was in the clubhouse.

No cleats. No pants.

We had to find him.

He threw on a pair of pants, laced up, and jogged out.

And he delivered.

Single to center.

Now the tying runs were on.

Two outs.

The crowd was roaring.

Ray Knight stepped in.

Blooped a single over second.

Carter scored.

Mitchell raced to third.

5-4.

The tying run was ninety feet away.

McNamara made a change. Brought in Bob Stanley.

NBC had already wrapped the Red Sox clubhouse in plastic. Champagne was on ice.

They were ready to celebrate.

Mookie Wilson stepped in.

Stanley's pitch wild.

Mitchell broke for home.

Safe.

5-5.

The stadium erupted.

I could feel Shea shaking. I thought the whole place might collapse from the noise.

NBC scrambled. Pulled the plastic. Packed up the champagne.

It wasn't over.

Ray Knight stood at second.

Mookie dug in.

Then he hit a slow roller to first.

Buckner bent down.

And the ball went under his glove.

"Holy shit!" I screamed.

Ray Knight raced home.

Bud Harrelson ran beside him, fist in the air.

We poured out of the dugout.

It was the most exciting game I'd ever seen—even though I left in the fifth.

We had hope.

We had another day.

After the game, Rafael, Junior, and I grabbed a bite.

I was exhausted. Emotionally drained.

"This is a future Hollywood movie," Junior said.

I laughed.

"It was the chain," Rafael said, grinning.

We all laughed.

"No," I said. "It was the baseball gods. They looked over us tonight."

We lived to see another day.

Act 90: The Rainout

"So, Game 7 was scheduled," Sonny said. "And then it was rained out. What did you do that day?"

"You're right," I said. "It was supposed to be played on Sunday, but the weather was bad. Real bad. The funny thing was, the New York Giants had a Monday Night Football game at the Meadowlands. So, we were going to be competing with a potential Super Bowl–bound team.

It was a great weekend for New York and New Jersey.

The game was pushed to Monday night.

Normally, I would have met up with Rafael and Junior. But for some reason, I drove out to Bellmore to visit my parents."

When I got there, my father was asleep upstairs. My mother was awake, sitting in the kitchen.

"Can you make your world-famous Bustelo coffee?" I asked.

She laughed and pulled out her **colador**—the old-school cloth strainer she always used. She boiled the water, spooned the coffee into the colador, and let the aroma fill the kitchen.

I remember the first time she said *colador*. I pictured a Mexican gangster with two six-shooters, ready for a standoff. And people scattering, saying, "Es el Colador."

I bought her a cappuccino machine a while back. It sat on the counter like a piece of furniture—untouched, ornamental. She never used it.

When the coffee was done, the caffeine cut through the grayness of the rain. I felt awake again.

I had about an hour's drive back to Manhattan, but I wasn't in a rush.

"Did my father see the game last night?" I asked.

"He did," she said. "He was tired today. Yesterday he invited some neighbors over. They watched the game with him."

I raised an eyebrow. "Wait. My father has friends? Is he on some kind of antidepressants?"

She laughed. "No. He actually has friends. He's happy with the car you bought him. He's always looking for an excuse to go food shopping or hit Walmart. He likes it here."

I didn't say anything. No smart remark. I just let her talk.

"You know what, Jervin?" she said. "He's proud of you. He was proud of Manny too."

She pointed to the folded flag on the mantle—the one they gave us when Manny died in uniform.

"He brags to his friends about you. You should have seen his reaction when Davey Johnson pinch-hit for you. I thought he was going to have an aneurysm."

I smiled. "Did he finish watching the game?"

"Oh yeah. I haven't heard him scream that loud since you broke the mirror when you were a kid."

I laughed.

"I'm glad he finally retired," she said. "He needed to enjoy his life."

"Is he inviting his friends over for tomorrow?"

"I think the whole neighborhood's coming. We're all going to cook. Make it an event. We're proud, Jervin. Your father especially. I know he doesn't show it, but you know how he is. He's old school. He bottles everything up."

I hugged her.

Then I hit the road.

On the drive back to Manhattan, all I could think about was my father's happiness. In the projects, he barely said a word to the neighbors. But in Bellmore, he was a social butterfly.

What a 360.

It made me laugh.

But my mind was already shifting.

Game Seven.

I didn't want to listen to the radio. I didn't want to watch the news.

This was the biggest game of my life.

And I didn't want any distractions.

Act 91: Game 7—The Final Showdown

"So, it's Monday," Sonny said. "Game Seven. The biggest game of your career. Tell us about it."

"The matchup was Bruce Hurst versus Ron Darling," I said. "Hurst had been masterful against us in Game 1. A little more hittable in Game 5, but sharp. He was not a fluke. He was a problem."

It was a damp, chilly evening. The kind of night where the cold seeps into your bones if you're not prepared.

This time, I remembered my long johns.

I wasn't about to let my knees freeze again.

But the first thrill of the night wasn't the weather or the matchup. It was hearing my name over the loudspeaker.

"Batting eighth and playing shortstop… number zero… Jervin Class."

The crowd roared.

And for a moment, I just stood there, letting it wash over me.

All the hours. All the setbacks. All of the nights I wondered if I'd ever make it. It was all worth it.

Just before I took the field for the last game of the year, I walked over to Bud Harrelson and gave him a fist bump.

"You were the man when I was a kid watching from the upper deck," I told him.

Harrelson smiled. "Now you're the man, kid."

He was one of the nicest men in baseball. He always had time for everyone. Always had a kind word. And tonight, he gave me something I didn't even know I needed.

A blessing.

I jogged out to shortstop.

The lights were bright. The crowd was deafening. The air was thick with tension.

Game Seven.

Let's dance.

Ron Darling was our starter.

He'd been great in Game 1—sharp, composed, surgical. In Game 4, he danced between the raindrops, but he got the job done. I always joked that Darling was the smartest guy on the team.

After all, he was an Ivy League graduate. You could see it in the way he carried himself—cool, analytical, unshaken.

When play started, the first batter was Wade Boggs.

He hit a liner right at me.

Routine.

But my heart was thumping. My adrenaline was pumping. I snagged it cleanly but felt like my glove was vibrating.

One out.

Next up was Marty Barrett.

The Shea crowd tried to rattle him—taunts, chants, the whole New York symphony. But Barrett had ice in his veins. He didn't flinch. Darling got him to ground out.

Two down.

Then came Buckner.

And something strange happened.

The Mets fans gave him a standing ovation.

A hero's welcome.

Only in New York.

Not too subtle.

Buckner tipped his cap, stepped in, and lined a single to right field.

Of course he did.

Top of the second.

Harry Albino

On a full count, Dwight Evans turned on a fastball and launched it deep into the night. The ball soared over the left-field wall.

Boston took the early lead, 1-0.

As Evans rounded the bases, I couldn't help but think back to the 1975 World Series. I was thirteen years old, watching him on TV. And now, here I was—on the same field, in the same game, facing the same man.

Baseball has a funny way of folding time.

Next up was Rich Gedman. He fouled one off down the right-field line, toward the makeshift stands we'd added for the Series. Fans reached for the ball—and the section gave way. The stands collapsed in a clatter of metal and limbs.

Thankfully, no one was seriously hurt.

The grounds crew rushed out to fix the damage. It took a few minutes. While they worked, I glanced over at the Red Sox dugout.

There, sitting on the edge, was Tom Seaver.

Eating sunflower seeds.

It looked… wrong.

Seaver in a Red Sox jacket? That was like seeing Sinatra in a Red Sox cap. It didn't sit right.

After the delay, Gedman stepped back in.

He hit a fly ball to right-center. Darryl Strawberry tracked it, reached up—and the ball bounced off his glove and over the wall.

Home run.

Just like that, it was 2-0.

It reminded me of Fenway when Lenny Dykstra hit one that bounced off Evans' glove. Baseball has a way of evening things out.

Darling walked the next batter, Dave Henderson.

Mel Stottlemyre came out to the mound. A rare visit. Our pitching had been solid all series. But this was Game 7. No room for hesitation.

With one out, Bruce Hurst came up to bunt. He dropped one down the third-base line. Ray Knight charged but overran it. Darling, always alert—former shortstop, elite fielder—scooped it up and made the play at first.

Two outs.

Henderson moved to second.

Then Wade Boggs slapped a grounder past me. I dove, but it was out of reach.

Henderson scored.

3-0, Boston.

Their dugout erupted. High fives. Laughter. That kind of energy that says, *we've got this.*

And who could blame them?

Then Marty Barrett bunted for a base hit.

I swear, that guy was killing us. Every time he came up, it felt like he had our number.

Davey Johnson wasn't wasting time. Sid Fernandez was up in the bullpen. One more run and this game could start slipping away fast.

Buckner stepped in.

This time, he flied out to Mookie in center.

I exhaled.

A small victory.

But the damage was done.

Top of the fourth.

Ron Darling hit Dave Henderson with a pitch. It wasn't intentional—just one that got away—but it brought a murmur from the crowd.

With one out, Bruce Hurst came up and laid down a textbook sacrifice bunt. Henderson moved to second.

Davey Johnson didn't wait.

He stepped out of the dugout and made the call.

Time for El Sid.

Sid Fernandez jogged in from the bullpen, all business. The crowd gave him a warm welcome. We needed him to stop the bleeding.

First batter—Wade Boggs.

Sid walked him.

But then he settled in.

Got Marty Barrett to pop out.

Inning over.

Sid was keeping us in the game.

Top of the fifth—he was electric. Fastball popping. Curveball biting. The crowd, which had been quiet since the second inning, started to stir again. You could feel the energy shifting.

Bottom of the sixth.

I led off.

Hit a grounder up the middle. Thought I had a chance. But Spike Owen ran over, made the play, and threw me out at first.

One down.

Lee Mazzilli came up to pinch-hit for Sid.

He rewarded Davey with a sharp single past Owen into left field.

Then Mookie Wilson lined a base hit to left.

Two on. One out.

McNamara had Steve Crawford warming in the bullpen.

The crowd was coming to life.

Tim Teufel stepped in.

Worked a walk.

Bases loaded.

The noise was deafening.

I loved every second of it.

Keith Hernandez came to the plate.

The captain.

He didn't wait around.

First pitch—line drive into left-center.

Mazzilli scored.

Mookie scored.

3-2.

Shea erupted.

Somewhere in the stands, I knew Rafael was turning to Junior and saying, "Now that's what I call a clutch hitter."

Same thing he said about Hernandez in Game 7 of the 1982 Series, when Keith came through with the bases loaded in the sixth.

Lightning, meet bottle.

Tim Teufel went from first to third on the hit. Davey pulled him and sent Wally Backman as a pinch runner.

Gary Carter stepped in.

He hit a bloop to right.

Dwight Evans came charging in—dove for it.

Nobody knew if he caught it or trapped it.

The ump hesitated.

Then signaled safe.

It was a hit.

But Hernandez had already rounded second and was caught in no-man's-land. He was tagged out trying to scramble back.

He argued the call—animated, frustrated. He knew the call was right. But he was sending a message.

On the play, Backman scored.

Tie game.

3-3.

Brand new ballgame.

Strawberry came up next, but he was retired.

End of the sixth.

We were heading into the seventh.

And Shea was shaking.

Top of the seventh.

Roger McDowell took over for Sid Fernandez. Sid had done his job—kept us in it—gave us a chance. Now it was McDowell's turn.

Tony Armas was sent up to pinch-hit for Bruce Hurst. That meant we'd be seeing Calvin Schiraldi in the bottom of the inning.

McDowell didn't flinch.

He shut Boston down. Quick work. No drama.

Bottom of the seventh.

Schiraldi on the mound.

Ray Knight led off.

On a 2-2 fastball, he turned on it—sent it soaring to left-center.

Gone.

The place erupted.

We came flying out of the dugout, nearly tripping over each other to mob Knight at home plate. It was chaos. Joyful, beautiful chaos.

I always found Knight to be a little arrogant. But he was a gamer. No denying that.

Next up, Lenny Dykstra pinch-hit for Kevin Mitchell.

Lenny slapped a single to right.

Boston tried a pitchout—expecting a steal—but Schiraldi airmailed the throw.

Dykstra took second.

I stepped to the plate.

Locked in.

I got a fastball and lined it down the first-base line. Clean.

Dykstra scored.

As I stood at first, I couldn't help but picture my father back in Bellmore, surrounded by his new friends, going crazy. I could almost hear him yelling at the TV, pounding the table, beaming with pride.

McDowell came up next and laid down a bunt, moving me to second.

McNamara made a move—brought in Joe Sambito.

Sambito didn't want any part of Mookie Wilson. He issued an intentional walk.

Then came Wally Backman, batting right-handed, his weaker side.

It didn't matter.

He worked a walk.

Bases loaded.

Keith Hernandez stepped in.

Second time in the game with the bags full.

He lifted a fly ball to deep left.

I tagged.

Took off.

Scored standing up.

6-3.

The crowd was in a frenzy. People were stomping, screaming, hugging. It felt like the whole stadium was levitating.

McNamara made another change—brought in Bob Stanley.

Stanley stopped the bleeding.

But the damage was done.

We were six outs away.

Six outs from history.

Top of the eighth.

The NYPD had parked on horseback in the bullpen.

I'd never seen that before.

Crowd control, they said.

Shea was on edge. Fifty-five thousand people holding their breath.

Buckner led off with a single to left.

Then Jim Rice smoked a bullet past me into left field. I barely had time to react.

Two on. No outs.

Davey Johnson got Jesse Orosco up in the bullpen.

Dwight Evans stepped in and ripped a double into right-center. Buckner scored. Rice scored.

Just like that, it was 6-5.

Boston was back in it.

Davey didn't hesitate. He walked to the mound and took the ball from McDowell.

In came Orosco.

I was told to play Evans tight at second. Cut his lead. Keep him honest.

Orosco bore down.

Struck out Dave Henderson.

Two outs.

McNamara sent up Don Baylor to pinch-hit for Spike Owen.
Baylor hit a grounder in the hole between short and third.

I ran over, backhanded it, and fired to first.

Got him.

Inning over.

I let out a long breath.

The key in those moments is not to panic. Just play the game.

Bottom of the eighth.

Al Nipper took the mound for Boston.

First batter—Darryl Strawberry.

Strawberry hit a towering shot over the right-center field wall.

7-5, Mets.

Strawberry did a slow trot around the bases. Back then, that was considered disrespectful. But this was Game 7. Emotions were raw.

Ray Knight met him at home plate. Pulled him aside. Said something—a reminder to stay humble. Knight was old school like that. Grew up with the Big Red Machine and future Hall of Famers.

Then Knight stepped in and singled.

His third hit of the night.

McNamara had seen enough. He ordered an intentional walk to me.

First and second. No outs.

Jesse Orosco came up.

He was supposed to bunt.

Instead, he bounced one up the middle.

Knight never hesitated. Rounded third and scored.

8-5.

The dugout was alive. The fans were alive. I was alive.

I turned to someone and said, "Orosco's gonna tell his grandkids he had an RBI single in the World Series."

Steve Crawford replaced Nipper.

As he warmed up, "We Will Rock You" by Queen blasted through the stadium speakers. Guys in the dugout were hugging, slapping backs, trying not to get ahead of themselves.

Crawford's first pitch hit Mookie Wilson.

Bases loaded.

Backman grounded into a force at home. Two outs.

Bases still loaded.

Keith Hernandez stepped in for the third time in the game with the bases juiced.

He hit a sharp grounder to Barrett at second.

Inning over.

But we'd done our damage.

We were three outs away.

Three outs from a championship.

If I said I wasn't excited, I'd be lying.

I was living my boyhood dream.

A dream very few get to live.

Top of the ninth.

Jesse Orosco on the mound.

Dances with the Dirt

Ed Romero was the first batter—he'd taken over for Spike Owen after the Don Baylor pinch-hit earlier. Romero hit a soft pop-up in foul territory. Keith Hernandez charged in from first and made the catch.

One out.

Two to go.

Next up—Wade Boggs.

Boggs hit a slow bouncer to Wally Backman. Wally scooped it clean and fired to Hernandez.

Two outs.

One more.

I glanced over at the Red Sox dugout.

The looks on their faces—I knew that feeling. The weight. The helplessness. The disbelief.

Then, out of nowhere, someone threw a smoke bomb.

We had to wait.

The field filled with haze. The umpires paused the game. The crowd buzzed, restless.

And then, slowly, the smoke cleared.

Literally.

Marty Barrett stepped to the plate.

Harry Albino

Boston's last hope.

Just like Carter had been ours in Game 6.

Barrett had been a thorn in our side. Clutch hits. Smart at-bats. Ice in his veins.

I looked over at our dugout.

Mayor Koch was there, standing just behind the railing, ready to celebrate with us.

The count ran full.

Two outs.

Barrett fouled one off.

Then Orosco delivered a slider on the outside corner.

Barrett swung.

Missed.

Strike three.

Orosco threw his glove into the air like a rocket.

The dugout exploded.

The players raced onto the field.

I placed my glove over my heart, pointed a finger to the sky, and whispered, "This is for you, Manny."

Then I ran.

Into the dogpile.

The NYPD were galloping their horses along the warning track like it was the Wild West. Fans were screaming, crying, climbing over each other. I've never seen so many grown men so happy in my life.

I looked over at the Boston dugout.

Wade Boggs was crying.

At first, I thought it was just the loss. But I remembered he'd lost his mother in a car accident earlier in the year.

This wasn't just a game for him either.

As I sprinted toward the clubhouse, champagne already in the air, I thought to myself—this is way better than the College World Series.

In the clubhouse, we drenched each other in champagne. Laughed. Cried. Screamed.

The commissioner stepped in and told us that President Ronald Reagan had called to congratulate us. He'd been watching the game. Of course he had—he was once a sports broadcaster. He loved this stuff.

Ray Knight was named Series MVP.

Deserved it.

But if there was an award for unsung hero, it would've gone to Sid Fernandez. No question.

Later that night, I called my mother.

"Ma, is Dad awake?"

"He's asleep," she said. "He wore himself out. He kept telling his friends this was better than 1969. And when you hit that single to drive in the run, he went crazy."

I didn't say anything at first.

I just let it sit.

I felt vindicated.

I felt like I'd finally earned something.

Recognition. Respect. A place in the story.

"I'll be there in a couple of days," I told her. "We've got a parade tomorrow."

Act 92: Canyon of Heroes

"So, without a doubt," Sonny said, "that was not only a thrilling run—it was like a Hollywood script. Tell us about the Canyon of Heroes."

It was early Tuesday morning.

I was driving downtown to get ready for the parade. For the first time in a month, I turned on the radio. I'd shut myself off from the world during the postseason—no TV, no papers, no distractions.

Now that it was over, I was ready to let it all in.

A caller on the radio said, "I see the Mets club as twenty-four jewels to a crown."

I thought that was poetic.

The team had told me I could have people on my float. So I invited Junior, Rafael, George, and Venus. At the last minute, Junior pleaded with me to include Carolyn.

I had no objection. I just didn't think she'd be interested.

Junior and Rafael had designed these beautiful leather jackets and T-shirts for the parade—part celebration, part promotion. They looked sharp. We looked like a team.

When I arrived downtown, I met up with my crew.

I turned to them and said, "I can't believe it. We're going to be paraded down the Canyon of Heroes. Like the 1969 Mets. Like the astronauts. That means we're going to have a plaque on the ground—for all of eternity."

The players started showing up. Handshakes. Laughter. Everyone was glowing.

Someone asked, "Where's Doc? Has anybody seen Dwight Gooden?"

People shrugged.

"Why isn't Gooden here?" Junior asked.

"I have no idea," I said.

About an hour later, we were on the float, waving to hundreds of thousands of fans who had packed the streets of Manhattan on a Tuesday morning.

As we rolled down Broadway, I put my arm around Carolyn.

"Isn't this great?" I said.

"Oh my God, I'm loving this," she said, eyes wide with joy.

"This is what you worked for, Jervin," Rafael said.

"Correction, Rafael," I told him. "This is what we worked for. Together. Without you or Junior, I never would've made it. I wanted you all here."

We waved and smiled. Fathers had their kids on their shoulders, just like when I was a boy. Music blared from every corner. Confetti rained down like ticker-tape snow.

At one point, I swore I saw someone in the crowd who looked like Anna.

Then again, there are a lot of women who look like Anna.

It didn't matter.

This was the best day of my young life.

I was on top of the world.

Sonny's voice returned, soft and steady.

"And with that, we're wrapping up Volume One of Jervin Class's story, entitled *Dances with the Dirt*. This is Sonny 'Mercury' Mercado, saying good night from *The Mercury Temperature*."

To Be Continued...